THE BRIGHT CANTONESE

I said, 'Answer me something. What are my
chances of coming back?'
'Your return is a certainty or I would not
be sending you.'
'The truth, Kwan.'
He examined the end of his cigarette. 'The
truth? About ten to one against.'
I took a deep breath. 'Peking accepts such
appalling odds?'
'Presumably. I have absolute clearance on
the assignment.'
I got up. Beyond the window the street was
brilliant with sunshine, the harbour deep blue
and crested.
'You are still prepared to go?'
A sickness rose in my throat and I swallowed
it down.
'Of course.'

The Bright Cantonese

Alexander Cordell

CORONET BOOKS
Hodder and Stoughton

Printed and bound in Great Britain for
Coronet Books, Hodder and Stoughton, London,
By C. Nicholls & Company Ltd,
The Philips Park Press, Manchester

ISBN 0 340 20803 1

For Jim Robinson

CHAPTER ONE

It is necessary at certain intervals to dye my hair: about this need I am reserved, so I do not often mention it. In the Extra-Murals of Peking University, which is the greatest in the world, there was a professor who would upbraid any girl seen using lipstick or dye, this being against the edicts of the Cultural Revolution. But when he saw me in the corridors he merely bowed.

Kwan To Lin, however, used to love my bright hair. He showed not the slightest embarrassment when seen with me in public; at the School of Espionage, despite his other faults, he was most careful to ensure that I received exactly the same treatment and privileges as the pure-blood Chinese students. There are some in this world who understand the predicaments of humans, and some who do not. Once he said to me:

"This is my woman, Mei Kayling, and she has hair like a wand of gold."

"It is shameful hair," I retorted, "it is not Chinese."

Smiling with slow charm, he said, "Is nationality important when one is making love?"

"It is important to know to whom one is making love. Soon I shall dye it."

At the door he said, "You will dye it when you are given permission, not before."

"You are going now?" I asked.

"Of course. I will meet you at the Hsin Chiao Hotel for the First Investigation."

"I will be there."

After Kwan had gone I sat at the bedroom table and stared into the mirror. The face that stared back at me was the face of a European. With the greatest care, and the aid of mascara, I changed my face into that of a Chinese.

Let lovers stop to think of the perfection of love, these

lovers of east and west who waste their words in dark places, mouth to mouth, in the honeyed sweetness of their loins and the panic of their breath.

Before they make Eurasians.

There is about the city of Peking in midsummer an air of triviality, of banter and gaiety that runs hand-in-hand with the gorgeous decoration which Nature sheds so bountifully. It is always a little astonishing to me that the blossoms blooming on the trees which we have planted since the Revolution bloom with equal brightness on the trees of the decadent west. The morning was flourishing with sweet air, the sky already glowing with the molten heat to come, as I paid off the boarding-house keeper.

The woman said, "One yuan fifty, missus."

I paid her, this little scramble of flesh out of old Honan. My green uniform with the armband of the Red Guard did not impress her, for she had seen the old chain-gang of the Kuomintang, and the sack of Canton.

"Your man has already gone?"

I replied, "My husband is concerned with the affairs of the Youth League: there is to be a big parade today, so he left early."

"There is much coming and going of husbands."

Peasants have the ability to be insulting without really trying.

Sunlight struck me in the face as I opened the door, adopting an air of unconcern, though Kwan was a fool, I reflected, to make this assignation so close to the city limits. For one destined to rise to high places he had little sense of social responsibility. The woman said:

"It is terrible, isn't it?"

"The accident in Kwangtung?"

She whispered, "The desecration of the graves."

"Such things are inevitable. In the search for absolute national purity all vestige of the old landed proprietors must be removed."

"Aye, but these are dead."

Kwan and I had heard them in the night, and listened, hand-in-hand. The new Red Guard movement finding its feet in eradicating the foul memory of China's travail. Kwan said it was a heresy of violence, but I did not agree. Bonfires had been lit in the streets, the headstones of the old European cemetery overturned. Chairman Mao himself had pledged his support to the new, violent movement: this was enough for me.

But the ancients of China still worship their ancestors: there is no way of changing such customs but to wait until they die out. I said to this woman:

"You are a good Communist?"

Her walnut face regarded me. "Ah, excellent."

"You told my husband that you came from the farms?"

"From Honan, many winters ago."

"And you remember the old Honan?"

"Every leaf, every bough, every starvation."

I replied, "Then you would marvel at the new Honan that the Red Guards have built. Do you know your Su Shiun?"

It frightened her, and was meant to. One can forgive presumption but not such intolerable impertinence.

"Who?" Her broken teeth leered from her shattered face, an appalling apparition made more dreadful by sun.

I said with command, "If you are a good Communist you are bound to know your Su Shiun. Now tell me," I quoted, " 'The soil. . . .' "

She said tonelessly, " 'The soil has ceased to belong to those who till it. And they who have the owning thereof . . .' " she faltered.

"Think, woman, think."

" 'And . . . and they who have the owning thereof toil not in the fields. Of their yield the landlord takes one half, for every ten farmers there is one proprietor.' "

"Excellent," I said. "I will tell my husband that despite your age you have a good memory."

She added, looking at nothing, "The Red Guards labour

with the harvest, they feed the people, they are the blood of China, and they rejoice in the glory of Chairman Mao's thoughts."

"Good day," I said.

There was little to be done with her, her generation was transitional. Steeped in gossip, scandalising and folk-lore, she was the epitome of old China: one moment enthusing about the gigantic success of the communes, the next burning paper money before her ancestral gods. But she also had a tongue.

It was cleaner in the street.

Violent with gay red streamers and plumes, the great coaches came hurrying down the wide boulevards of Tien An Men, crammed with students coming to attend yet another gala day of rejoicing. Vaguely, I wondered who it was this time: we were wooing the east. Afro-Asians in gorgeous saris strolled by in graceless excitement, their white-palmed hands jabbering in fine frenzy below the white flash of their teeth; their men darker and sultry with sun, expensively dressed in European suits. Probably Somaliland, I reflected — she had not been in Peking for a considerable time, and I wondered at the wisdom of these lavish entertainments. It was rather like fiddling while Rome was burning, as the Europeans say. Now a cavalcade of cars was coming from the city airport, and the crowds lining the square swayed and rippled with the wind of excitement. I paused, watching. It was the processional hymn of everlasting friendship, a proclamation that the east was Red: the tambourines and Asian dances of the students who jigged with false delight to the diplomatic hand-waving and bows of the visiting dignitaries — all this but a tinsel decoration that covered the face of national grief: ten thousand dead in the province of Kwangtung. Ten thousand dead and many thousands blinded. I closed my eyes. It was a national calamity for which the scientists would pay with their lives. And amid the growing clamour of the crowds I pushed my way on, seeing in the eye of my mind a shattered Canton, her skeleton timbers rearing in blackened desolation through the plumes of fire.

I reached the edge of the fantastic Tien An Men square. Here the students paraded. The scarf-dance of the falling harvest was in full swing, and the wheat fell obliquely to the scythe: a swathe of ten thousand children laying themselves flat on their faces as a giant blade of silver moved among them. The crowd roared. Distantly, on the balcony before the Great Hall of the People, I saw our beloved Chairman Mao and flung out my hands to him, shrieking his name. The loud-speakers shattered the morning, the martial music roared to a higher note. Doves rose in a white cloud above Tien An Men, scattering themselves into a molten sky like a handful of shavings flung into the wind. Lin Piao I saw, and Chou En-lai, the leaders of the Cultural Revolution, the heroes of the Long March. Like the crowd I shrieked with joy, banishing my thoughts of burning Kwangtung. A million people roared their loyalty into the beauty of the morning, and their devotion to Mao Tse-tung.

I looked at my watch. It was nearly ten o'clock.

Kwan was waiting on the steps of the Hsin Chiao hotel, as I expected.

I nodded briefly. He was in one of his damn-fool moods and I didn't like it.

He asked, "Did you rest well, Mei Kayling?"

I said, walking past him, "Not as I had hoped. The lodging was noisy, the politics poor by peasant standards and the company bourgeois-intellectual."

"Did you report this?"

Over my shoulder I said, "I might even do that," and added, "Actually, I spent most of the night awake."

It delighted him and he smiled, saying, "Somebody else must have had the enjoyment."

"Have the others come?" I ignored this rudeness.

"They have been here six minutes. You are late."

"I am sorry. The crowds in Tien An Men."

I followed him into the foyer. To me it seemed a ridiculous place for a conference. This was eminently a hotel for foreigners, though none, I noticed, seemed to be around today. Kwan said:

"Where is your suitcase?"

"At the People's Hostel."

"But you did not spend last night at the People's Hostel."

"Don't be a fool, Kwan, send for it."

There stand, above the crimson foyer of the Hsin Chiao, two life-sized figures of China Revived: they stared at me with blank eyes, and condemnation. Coming up the stairs behind me Kwan said:

"It is inconceivable that beneath those green trousers walk the most beautiful legs."

In this mood he was dangerous. I smiled, walking on, returning bows.

"Uniforms," he said softly, "are a form of treachery. They induce in the old an unwarranted dignity. Simplified, they add inches to a man's political stature — our own leaders are a terrifying example. But to women they do the most dreadful things, especially trousers."

I ignored him, but it was frightening. Kwan was versed in the freedoms and scope of the new institutions. He was principal of the Junior School of Espionage, and this, I supposed, allowed him almost unlimited licence of expression. Mine was limited. As a Student of Espionage, second-class and but recently graduated, there was, for me, the hidden microphone. Behind every one of the ten million trees they have planted since the Revolution there is, it is said, an eye.

At the top of the stairs I turned to the right.

"This way," said Kwan, and opened a door.

A man was sitting at a table; he was alone in the small room.

This was the Second Investigator; the First Investigation would come later, in Council.

Do not let them frighten you, Kwan once said. Such investigations, which come automatically before every pro-

12

ject, are relegated to the crusty old heroes of the Long March who call into the Intelligence Department before being transferred to minor positions in the Party Organisation. But Kwan, I was to find, though right in so many things, was quite wrong in this.

The man at the table was old: his head was bald, a skull screwed on to a hairless neck, his teeth projecting over bloodless lips. Yet his voice, when he spoke, was strangely beautiful, coming from a crack in the coffin of his soul.

"Mei Kayling?"

"1869681, Mei Kayling, Red Guard, Second Class."

"Please come in." He waved a hand and I sat to attention before him.

"You know why you are here?"

"Yes, Investigator."

He folded his hands on the desk before him, motioned Kwan to a chair, and said, "But you do not know in detail?"

"She knows nothing in detail," said Kwan.

"I am referring my remarks to the woman Mei. You have a tongue of your own?" he asked me.

"Yes, Investigator."

"Then use it. Where were you born?"

"In Hong Kong."

"How long did you live there?" He began to write, a slow, precise hand.

"For two years only."

"How old are you, Mei Kayling?"

"Twenty-four."

"And your parents are dead, it says here."

I nodded, glancing at Kwan. He was sitting with his legs crossed, his face betraying his usual boredom. Nothing infuriated him more than the intensity of aged officialdom. Had Kwan been given his head I should have been on the 'plane south by now, but this was sheer stupidity. The Party knew my history down to the most trifling detail. The Investigator said:

13

"I have your record here, woman. In your own words state it again, that I may check it with the official history."

Kwan said instantly, "Investigator. When we have finished here she has the First Investigation in Council to face. Everything is before you. I myself recommended this woman on the basis of that record."

"Then if she states her own history she will know it that much more clearly, will she not?"

"She has stated it every week in the School of Espionage for the past two years."

"So you identify her?"

"As my most brilliant pupil."

"Excellent. But brothers, under certain circumstances, have the greatest difficulty in identifying sisters; husbands are equally remiss with wives; and lovers, Kwan To Lin, are the most untrustworthy of the lot."

I closed my eyes. Sweat flooded to my face as I remembered the boarding-house keeper, the woman of Honan. The Investigator said, and I dared not look at Kwan:

"It matters little, Mei Kayling. The amorous nature of your tutor in no way denies the brilliance of his espionage. State your record."

I began obediently, with the intonation of a parrot:

"My name is Mei Kayling. I am the daughter of a Chinese mother and a British father. I have a sister living, her name is Chieh, and she is of pure Chinese blood, being two years older than me. When my father died my mother took us to live in Macau, and there Chieh and I worked in the fire-cracker factories of a Portuguese imperialist. When I was ten years old we moved to the village of Hoon, which is north of Canton in the province of Kwangtung. I was top of my class in the school of Sun Commune, and on my twelfth birthday a letter came from the Government calling me to Canton Middle School for further education. . . ."

The Investigator interjected, "But for reasons best known to herself your mother sent your sister Chieh to Canton Middle School, with your papers."

"That is correct, Investigator."

"And then?"

"Within three days the authorities had sent my sister back to Hoon. She could not pass the entrance examination."

"Pray continue."

I heard Kwan sigh, and I said, "My mother did nothing for a month, then a letter came from the Canton authorities demanding that she should appear before the elders of Hoon village: that she should explain her reasons for trying to educate the wrong child. . . ."

"What followed after this?" The Investigator examined my record with scrupulous care.

In better words than these I told him, words that had become a part of a life-long explanation of my birth, my countenance, my hair; something like this I told him:

That they sat cross-legged in a half-circle before me, these Hoon elders. With impassive eyes they sat while I stood with my mother on trial. And around me, the greatest degradation of all, stood the village children, fingers in their mouths, eyes wide with the expectation of a public execution, the victim a mongrel bitch with long, golden hair.

"You sent the wrong child to Canton School, woman?" asked an Elder.

My mother clutched herself, saying, "It is a sad story and I am most embarrassed."

"You will be more embarrassed if the Government institutes an inquiry. What is this child's name?"

"By my name she is a Wong; in English it is Warren, the name of her English father. Shall I be punished?"

"Does one beat a donkey for mating with a horse? What name do you call her?"

"Mei Kayling. Out of shame I gave her this name."

The wind whispered about us, blowing my bright hair over my face. The watching children nudged each other; women whispered behind their hands.

"Where was she conceived?"

"In Spring Garden Lane, a roof-top in Hong Kong."

"You later married this Englishman?"

"After she was born. He was going to take us to England, but when she was two years old he died."

"So she was born a bastard?"

My mother raised her face. "Women starve before men in Hong Kong. It is not the first time the womb has saved the stomach, so do not look so saintly."

"Do not be impudent. Confine yourself to replies or you will appear before the Commune Director. Why did you not send this Mei Kayling to Canton as you were ordered? Why send the loutish sister?"

"It was enough that I was shamed before my village. When she was born this girl was dark; later her hair grew white, her complexion changed, her eyes became blue. With this straw hair and disgusting face – how would my name stand in the great city of Canton? Would you have me parade this degradation?"

At this the elders conferred, wiggish, waggish, shaking their heads.

Then one said, "So legally she is English."

"That is her nationality under English law."

"That is not a nationality, woman, that is a punishment!"

Forgetting me, they bellowed at this. Even my mother laughed, rocking and stamping about while I stood motionless, fighting to obliterate the shame. Then one, a younger man, cried:

"Let us be clear on this. This mother had a problem. How could she send an English child to be educated at the expense of the Chinese people?"

"But she is not all English."

"She is a half-and-half. But one thing is certain – she is brilliant and China needs brilliance. And she has Chinese blood – no, stop laughing, I beg you – it is important to the child. Some name and nationality must be entered for the record, if she is going to Canton School. But which? Is she a Wong or is she a Warren?"

The chief said, "Just tell everything. Tell the truth as we

16

see it – too many lies have been told already. They will sort it
out when she gets to Canton," and he took up his brush and
wrote with the greatest care, his tongue between his teeth:

'Female aged twelve years: name Mei Kayling in China
and May Warren in England. Father British but dead, a man
of the sea. Mother Chinese. Nationality unknown to us in
Hoon Sun Commune. Country unknown to us, believed
stateless. Hair golden straw, eyes strangely light: probably
albino. Forwarded for further education, being outstanding.
Canton authorities please assist.'

After writing this the elder turned to my mother, saying:

"Why is this child crying? Tell her not to be ridiculous."

"She possesses," said my mother, "this blue book. In it is
her photograph, also one of me. Her father obtained this blue
book for us from the Hong Kong Government, when he was
going to take us to England."

The Investigator straightened at the desk before me, and
held up the passport.

"This blue book, Mei Kayling?"

"One like that," I answered. "For on my sixteenth birthday, under the instruction of Central Intelligence, I visited
Hong Kong with my mother and renewed the passport, in my
own name."

The Investigator smiled at Kwan. "Not in your time,
perhaps, Kwan To Lin, but excellent forethought: much
credit devolves upon your Department." He turned again to
me. "A remarkable beginning, Mei Kayling. Will you proceed from there?"

"I will proceed from there, Investigator," said Kwan
hastily. "Her identity is surely proved. After three years in
Canton Middle School she became First Pupil, gaining
certificates in French and English literature. Both languages
she now speaks fluently, as well as the Cantonese dialect of
the area near Hoon."

"A most necessary qualification for the project. Please go
on."

Kwan continued, "Called to Peking University in the summer of 1959, she there graduated in Chinese Classical History and Agricultural Science by Mechanisation, and performed much research into commune methods. Since leaving university she was first employed in the office of Cultural Affairs, where she received grounding in European habits, customs and manners. For the past two years she has been instructed in the School of Espionage – latterly under my personal tutorage." He smiled faintly. "Member of the Red Guard, Second Class: politically sound, anti-revisionist, fanatically loyal . . ." he murmured ". . . Aren't we all?"

When I reached the door the Investigator said:

"How old were you when your mother died, Kayling?"

"Seventeen. We were living in Macau."

"You visit her grave?"

"Out of duty, Investigator."

"China needs you today. It is a different China now, my child."

I saluted and left the chamber, following Kwan down a crimson, thick-piled carpet to a lonely room.

"Wait here," he said.

I entered this room and sat clutching the passport, staring at the swaying crowds in the flower-lined road below me. For the first time fear was replacing nervousness. They knew about me in the most astonishing detail; they knew when I slept and rose; they knew the intimate processes of my thoughts. As Kwan left the room I had given him a look betraying my disgust at his utter stupidity. Knowing all this, knowing the investigations to come, he had exposed himself, and me, to the highest suspicion and danger. This project was bigger than him, me, or a million like us: it was as big as China herself. The door opened and Kwan returned, saying lightly:

"The last investigation awaits you, Miss May Warren."

"You fool," I whispered, "you knew all this, yet you risked us both last night. You realise what will become of us if this leaks out?"

"Let the punishment take its course," said he. "Your head,

too, my sweet – not only mine will fall. For while the Party advocates the highest degree of social relationship between individuals it takes two, Kayling, to make it sexual."

To appear before the First Investigation in Council it was necessary to cross the Tien An Men, which was an experience in itself that morning. I followed Kwan through the packed crowds, shouldering a path through the deafening cheers of Red Guards, for the scarf-dance was still in progress: a quarter of a million of Peking's youth in a fantastic jubilation of colour, the fluttering scarves weaving ornate and lovely patterns against a backcloth of orange, red and gold; a mammoth repetition, I reflected, of the giant caravanserais that lurched on gilded camels along the old silk route beyond Urumchi in Sinkiang. Oh, this beloved Peking! The old Chungtu and a thousand years before! Sacked by Genghis Khan and burned by Kublai Khan, the flames melting it into the Great Tatu. Peiping during the Ming dynasty, old when London was a hamlet; ravaged and looted by the Golden Horde, raped by conquerors, destroyed by earthquake, risen from the ashes of tyranny she stands today as the apex of China's politics, culture and love. My heart beat faster as I watched her in this new glory: for this great mother it would be a privilege to die.

"Hurry!" called Kwan, and I followed him swiftly up the marble steps of the Great Consortium; now through the swing doors of kruen and gilt and on to the cold mosaic of the Great Hall of the people. Down corridors we went, my steel-tipped boots echoing. We paused. Kwan's face was pale, I noticed.

The woman Mei, *the woman Mei!*

Whispers, hushed replies, messengers on tiptoe coming and going.

"This way," said Kwan.

Flanked by giant Red Guards of Shansi, we entered an ornate and beautiful room. Kwan took a seat beside me; together we faced a semi-circular table and three elderly men, all dressed in the green of the Red Guard.

19

"Greetings, Kwan To Lin, Red Guard Mei Kayling."

"Greetings."

It was instant; no preparations; time was precious.

"You are known in the Guard as The Bright Cantonese?" This from the youngest of the Committee, his face expressionless.

Kwan's voice rang loud and clear, and he delighted me.

"By this name is she known in the Junior School of Espionage, comrade, not in the Guard."

"My apologies, Mei Kayling."

"She has not been briefed?" asked another.

"She has not been briefed," said Kwan. Papers were shuffled at this, the turning point in the business. Distantly I heard the roar of the crowds from Tien An Men.

"But she knows of the disaster in Kwangtung?"

"Of this I have informed her," answered Kwan.

"She will now hear the detail." He turned to me. "Kayling, four days ago, at two minutes past midday, more than ten thousand people died in Kwangtung Province. Thousands more were blinded. These are estimates, and they are conservative, for the situation there is changing from minute to minute. The ratio of blindness to death is approximately three to one. The province is under martial law, first aid teams are being flown in, food and medical aid are being despatched by land and sea." He raised his sallow face to mine. "The cause of this disaster is not yet known. No speculation has been made, none will be tolerated. Like the other leaders we have sent south your mind will doubtless fly to nuclear fission. I beg you to dismiss this possibility: at this level it is we who do the thinking; your task is to appreciate the immediate situation and put the remedies in hand. Central Intelligence has absolutely no proof of a hostile act, nor of the cause of the catastrophe."

He rose at the desk. "You will proceed by 'plane to the air-strip at Hoon, which is your village in Sun Commune. You know this country, I understand."

"Perfectly," I replied.

"And you know the way through the mountains to the south?"

"I do."

He said, "Our hospitals are overflowing. The orders of the Central Committee are that your people will be taken to Hong Kong, where hospitals are available. You will command a party of eight hundred."

Kwan looked up. "Border protection, comrade?"

"There will be none. Hong Kong belongs to China. When China chooses she will use Hong Kong, and she chooses now. Border resistance will be swept aside; incidents will be immediately reported to Peking."

Another said with slow officialdom, "Party of eight hundred, men, women, children; Route Four, through Chung Mountains, leader the woman Mei Kayling."

The spokesman said, "And now a pledge to secrecy. Fifteen columns are under orders, fifteen leaders have been briefed. It is admitted that it does not require a student of espionage to take a stumbling people into Hong Kong – this could be done by the most illiterate of snakeheads. You will see that there is a higher cause involved."

I glanced at Kwan. It was inconceivable that he had not known all this last night: amid the sighs, the great tell-tale emotion of love, all this he had known, yet not imparted by a glance or breath. The assignment spokesman said:

"Of those fifteen most are interchangeable – six men, nine women. Of the women the most important is the Guard Mei Kayling: of the men the most important are Kwan To Lin, the Japanese Ku Ata, and Lum. There is a main stream of espionage, there is the subsidiary. You have the individual briefs, Kwan To Lin?"

Let me be clear on this: Kwan was not Red Guard. Though head of the Junior School of Espionage, he was junior to the Central Espionage. And there was in this room the detectable gap between the military and the civilian. Kwan's apparent boredom was directed to the dais as part of the eternal disdain which he showed for militarism: the

21

assignment spokesman, in his turn, treated Kwan with that overburdening politeness which, done well, can fringe on insult.

"I have the briefs, Investigator," said Kwan at nothing.

"Excellent, I will take them." With calculated coldness the spokesman reached out, took them, and placed them on the desk before him, adding: "By memory Kwan To Lin will brief you individually; this is the quality we demand, and get." He smiled faintly. "What Party is yours, Kwan To Lin?"

"Number Two, comrade."

"And the route you take?"

"Route Seven."

"You will rendezvous with the woman Mei Kayling in Hong Kong?"

"Only through an intermediary."

"You trust this person?"

"You placed him, comrade; our lives are in your hands," Kwan said at the ceiling. "And now a question, Investigator."

The room was stilled. His voice appeared to echo in the vaults above us, a strange timbre of challenge.

"Proceed."

Kwan said, "I challenge the validity of this planning, I challenge its sense. It is invalid because it is against the precepts of the teaching: it is nonsense because old practices and proved successes have made it nonsense. We are trained in the parachute, we are distance swimmers under-water. We have learned to move unobserved by night, the country swallows us by day. Since when, Investigator, did our espionage move in the herd?"

It was a tremendous impact on officialdom. The men at the table moved uneasily, then one, the eldest, rose and said:

"Kwan To Lin, we acknowledge your status, but you must acknowledge our wisdom. Hong Kong is unharmed, it is close to Routes Four and Two, it is on the march that will be taken by the Japanese Ku Ata, and Lum. When Hong Kong

22

needs water China supplies water, or Hong Kong would die. Now is Hong Kong's opportunity to repay – to nurse some of our sick and injured." He paused, staring about him. "Further, you must know this. Eight agents were sent into Hong Kong recently, none have returned, and it is presumed that they are lost. . . ."

"And you hope to get agents over the Shamchun River under cover of the refugees, comrade?" This from Kwan, now standing.

"It has been done before. Kwan To Lin, this is policy, not espionage. The espionage begins when you and your agents are safely delivered."

"And are not the British now warned?" asked Kwan. "What was successful in the past will most surely fail in the future, and this is China's future!"

The Investigator said, "Let this be known to you, and the assembly. There are but two men in China who can foretell China's future. We, the lesser men, protect her present. I counsel you, be obedient."

Kwan said, "Then tell these two men of me, Investigator, when they lead me out to the wall."

I could have shouted for the joy of knowing him. The Investigator bowed.

Sweat beaded on my forehead and I wiped it into my hair.

"Come," said Kwan softly.

We were the first to leave, in admonishment: this, I thought, was a time to pray to gods.

Our boots echoed on the cold mosaic; commands rang out, the gilt doors crashed behind us.

"Move in the herd," whispered Kwan. "Idiocy is the stamp of age. What fool people!"

With the sun-blaze of Peking flaring in the doorway we went through the Consortium into the terror of the day. It was midsummer, yet I was shivering: it was strangely cold.

CHAPTER TWO

The village elders were waiting for me on the little airstrip at Hoon, a thousand miles farther south. These, the leaders of the commune who once had judged me, now stood in clutched anguish, staring at the young Red Guard. Leaping down from the little aeroplane and dragging my bundle after me, I said:

"I am Mei Kayling, the leader of Party Six, Route Four, through the Chung mountains."

They whispered among themselves in awe. Many had bandaged hands and faces, one peered at me through the burned slits of his eyes: for this was Sun Commune, the fringe area of the disaster.

"You have papers, woman?"

The pilot of the aeroplane came up behind me. "She has papers but I will guarantee her; she is from Social Security."

I looked about me, seeing, for the first time in years, the familiar outline of a blazing country and the mackerel clouds shimmering above the peaks of mountains. Once it was a starving land, then honeyed, until the Great Light came. The refugees pressed about me.

"How many people have you got?" I asked.

"Seven hundred and eighty-two."

"They have been fed?"

"They have been fed and watered according to the radio instructions."

"Are they all from Hoon?"

"No, Red Guard. Many are from the south, on the road to Myen."

Most were burned; many more had charred clothing.

"None are blind," said the elder. "Although they saw the Big Light in the mountains, none are blind."

Another cried in a strange falsetto, "You know the dialects, Peking girl?" He nudged his neighbour.

I replied: "I know the dialects. Do you not remember the bright Cantonese?"

This quietened them and they whispered, gesticulating, pointing at my arm-band of the Guard, staring at my hair.

I said, moving among them, "How far is it to the Hong Kong border?"

"Eighty miles as the black duck flies."

I looked at the sky. Heat poured down in flashes, striking at my face. The people moaned, rocking with their burns.

"You will rest first?"

"Tell the people to find shade," I answered. "We will move at dusk."

There is, in Red China, the intellectual and the peasant; those who command and those who obey. And the crowd faltered to the shrieked commands of the commune leaders, then gathered up their belongings and ran for shade. But one woman stayed, a child clutching at her skirts. She said:

"I was at the door when the Big Light came."

"Was this south, near Canton?"

"At Myen. The men were in the fields, the children in school. The Mechanisation Brigade had come for the first reaping. I had gone to the door to call my son, Hu Han. He answered, I think, and I shut the door to keep out the sun. When the Light came the window blazed and the mountains went on fire. It scorched my eyes."

"You were looking towards the mountain?" I asked.

"The north window faces the mountains, and these caught fire."

An elder said, "She insists that the Great Light came from the mountains, and that is ridiculous."

"From where, then?" I asked.

"From the valley where the atomic laboratories lie; this is the work of scientists."

I shrugged him away. It was interesting to get another point of view, but I was not prepared to argue the merits of scientists. I said to the woman:

"And your son — what about your son?"

"His eyes burned dead in his face. My son stayed in Myen. Like the six men of the Mechanisation Brigade — blind."

"The Government will take action against the scientists," said the elder. "It is madness to plan tests of nuclear fission in a populated area."

"The Big Light," said the woman, "came from the mountains. . . ."

I took her arm. "Come."

Later, with the elders bleating like sheep about them, with the Youth League of Hoon herding them along, I took the column south.

Next day, with the sun high, a man came from the column and jogged along at my elbow. He spoke, but at first I ignored him, then he said:

"Red Guard, are you in charge of water?"

"I am in charge of everything."

"Ah Wen, the cripple of Hoon — his father has borrowed water."

I did not like these people. Many years ago, some with their blood had watched my agony in the square of Hoon, and not lifted a finger to save a child: now the child was leading them. Faintly, above the tramp of feet, I heard a cry.

The sun was sinking as I knelt on the pass, tending a girl whose knee was sliced open. Her name was Annoi and she was six years old. The blood gushed hot over my fingers, for the big vein was cut. Although I held the pressure point the blood would not congeal.

"Do not cry," I said, "it is unwomanly to cry." And then I remembered the cripple of Hoon and rose, shouting: "Send to me the father of the cripple Ah Wen!"

This happened on the pass of the mountain between Fatshan and Kongmoon, not twenty miles from Hoon airstrip. The man came to me with his baby in his arms. I said, bandaging, not looking up:

26

"Is your name Wen?"

"Ah."

I could have told him his name. Age had withered him, though above the knees he was still a handy-man: seventy if a day, and the child of his loins was six months old. This was the elder who had written my name, and called me half-and-half. Now I said:

"Is it true that you have borrowed water?"

"Aye. I borrowed water from my friend Sha Min."

The girl whimpered under my hands. I held her flat with my forearm and strained at the bandage.

"Did you not fill up your jar at Hoon?"

"My girl-wife weeps for water, she is making milk."

"Then why did you not bring double jars? Fool! You call yourself an elder?"

He stared down at me. I saw the opaque film over his pupils; hunger strolled in the caverns of his face; he drooped before me, rags fluttering in a hot wind. I said, "Do you remember me, Wen?"

He held the child closer, shaking his head.

"You do not remember the bastard of Hoon, the bright Cantonese?"

His eyes widened momentarily. I rose, shouting down the drooping line of people, "You see this fool here? He has borrowed water. He calls himself a leader, yet he borrows water. But the bigger fool is the man who lent it. You hear me down there?"

Intimidated, scarecrowed by heat, they stared at me in the stricken manner of the peasant. I cupped my hands to my mouth and yelled, "The next one to borrow water I will send back to Hoon airstrip. And the next one who lends it I will flog on a tree, even elders."

They stared at me with sullen eyes.

"Right, move!" I cried.

Kongmoon, shattered and derelict, winked in the darkness from five hundred feet below, and in that darkness another came and walked beside me at the head of the column.

"There is a girl, and her name is Yen-Sa," he said. "Trouble, woman."

Six feet if an inch, this one, with bull shoulders on him.

"What of this girl?" I did not spare him a glance.

"She is walking, and she is in labour."

I had seen this girl in the compound at the Hoon airstrip, the other women bundling about her, denying her shape.

"Tell her to bite her lips," I said. "We stop at midnight, not before."

Night pulled the blankets over her head, the plains below me glittered moon-dust after the incinerating heat of the day. And the big Kwantung moon dropped her samfoo trousers and sat her great white backside on the rim of the China hills. The people slept savage, in owl-shriek and curved beaks of tormenting dreams, under the quick-fire stars.

I saw his face in the blue light.

"My name," he said, "is Yuen Sun Johnny."

My first impulse was to order him back to the people. He watched me, half smiling, insolence brooding on his mouth. He had stripped to the waist and there was a smell of sweat and tobacco about him. Kwan once smelled like this, I remembered, in the commune outside Peking, when the students helped with the harvest.

"From her loins she brought a girl," he said.

"I heard her cry."

She had been crying for an hour and I had cursed her; holding my stomach I had sat on the rocks, labouring with her.

"It is bad luck," he said. "Much better to birth a boy."

"That is for Old China," I retorted. "This is New China."

"Freedom, food, equality?" he asked.

I did not reply. The girl Yen-Sa must be sleeping, I reflected. I hated her immorality; the difference between virtue and vice being the ability to remain undiscovered.

"You sleeping?"

"Later, perhaps," I replied.

28

He stretched out his long legs and grunted deep. "You come down special from Peking University to lead us people into Hong Kong?"

I nodded. His presence was disturbing me. There was a great loneliness in me for Kwan.

"What you doing up in the big university, girl?"

"Studying agriculture, and do not call me girl."

"O, aye?" He grinned at the moon. "You'm wasting time learning agriculture. What we want is a whip to the sky. Three months long we got no rain in Hoon and the people start praying to the old gods, but the land was dead long 'fore that."

"You criticise the Revolution?" I sat up instantly.

He shrugged his great shoulders. "I blame the intellectuals; too much writing and no digging."

He needed watching. This was the new peasantry. Out of confidence they were born, straight-limbed, wide-eyed and alert, and they were fed. If a counter-Revolution came it would be led by such as these. I said:

"Brain for the writing, brawn for the fields. You do the digging. The thinking will be done by your betters."

He warmed to me. "That's what we done. Me and my family are good Communists. We barned up the new fertiliser the Party sent down, we dug it in and planted rotation like the paper said, and we hoed up. But this is on paper, and it don't rain. The crop don't rise, the fellas get stalked in the sun. You from Hoon, they tell me?"

"I am from Hoon."

"Then you know that sun. We dug the canals and they come dry."

I replied, looking away, "It all takes time. Kwangtung is like this; an excess of rain, or drought. She has been like this for four thousand years. We are studying ways of bringing rain."

"You should get movin'." He winked. "You know Sun Commune, then?"

"Like my hand."

"We dug the canals deep, drilled wells, built a power house

29

— you show me a commune south of Canton that built a power house from scrap generators. With the electricity we drove water-wheels. We got Chinese cabbage, rice, wheat, sweet potatoes, but we starved come winter — no rain come summer."

"And you blame the Party for that?"

"I blame the Party for wasting our time."

"Is that fair?"

"We got to blame someone."

I said, my voice rising, " 'There is an end to darkness. The salvoes of the October Revolution bring us Marxism-Leninism. The great May Movement raises the standard for opposing imperialism and feudalism. The Chinese Communist Party is born!' "

He scratched his ear, staring at me. "But we still got no rain."

"You know your doctrines? You read the pamphlets?"

"Aye."

"Then you will know that your trust and loyalty must be unquestioned. The thought of Chairman Mao illumines all!"

There was a silence between us. The wind blew hot from the charred timbers of Kongmoon; the skeleton farms gaped up at the moon. Yuen Sun Johnny said, "You believe all this?"

"Every line, every word. The Party will move mountains, it will alter the course of the rivers, change the tides, and bring rain, all in good time."

"And where were you in '62 when we up and run for Hong Kong like now, in famine?"

"I was in Peking."

He got up, stretching himself, looking magnificent, and said, "And I was here and I watched the people starve. I ran with the rest of them to Hong Kong and the guards turned us back, like they will do this time. Anything goes wrong and we run for Hong Kong. Last time we got drought and famine, this time we got a Big Light, so we run again, an' we got Red Guard intellectuals like you sent down to lead us."

I rose, facing him. This is the trash that hangs on the legs

30

of New China; the pseudo-Communist who snaps at the heels of progress.

He grinned, saying, "You hope to get this lot through the border post without machine-guns?"

"I shall get them through."

He spat past me. "Then you'm a better woman than I give credit for, Peking girl. You get this lot into Hong Kong and I'll string my backside six feet high on any peg of the Party." He turned and went down the pass.

I leaned my face against the rock, wondering how Kwan would have handled it.

CHAPTER THREE

At sun-go-down next day the people wanted to rest, but I kept them moving over the flat land: it was a running, reviling exhibition of command, but I kept them going. By dusk they were jogging beside me at the head of the column, begging with their hands. One more mile I squeezed out of them in argument before I halted the snakehead.

"Camp!" I shouted, and they sank down where they had stopped, showing each other their blistered feet, threatening with their fists up. Some had brought compass paradise pointers, and these they placed on the track, calling to each other the true north and saying I was wrong in my direction: some even shouted that I was a Hong Kong snakehead, accusing me of leading them back into China, and for this it was death by hanging. All this was brought on by weariness and thirst, for it had not rained. No rain had fallen since the beginning of the march, and the water-jars were empty. In that moonlight the people moaned and rocked against each other. Removed from them I sat alone against a boulder and watched the stars. I ached. My feet were fire. And in that loneliness a man came to me, one Sung Po. He came with confidence and with hatred in his face. Once a compradore in old Honan, the Party had stripped him of his wealth and

31

imprisoned him for cruelty to the people. Now a convert to the cause of Communism, he stood before me on the track with the tireless chagrin of one who changes his coat.

"Before me in my dream," he said, "I saw a child fall, and a snakehead hanging on a tree."

I replied, "In your compradore shop you made good Honan wine, they tell me."

"You mock me? Young Red Guard, I tell you this: I dreamed of death."

There are many like these in China, the refuse of the Revolution; human nature is strange. The body can withstand privation and torture, but take the money out of its pocket and the brains come out of the head. I looked beyond him to the next rim of mountains, the bastion that guards Hong Kong.

"Soon it will rain," I said.

"The child of Yen-Sa is dead," he whispered.

I rose, staring into his haggard face.

"When?"

"On the march. The baby died of heat. It is a terrible omen. Also I saw a child fall and a snakehead hanging from a tree."

"Has the child been buried?"

"The men are doing it now. Do not fear the men, fear the women, Mei Kayling."

I said, "I have a task. I have sworn to take this column into Hong Kong. I will lose no lives doing this, but I take no account of new births. She should never have joined the march at Hoon."

"Tell that to the women," he said, and left me.

"And send the women to me one by one," I shouted. "No woman sleeps until I have seen her."

"It will be a popular decision," said Sung Po over his shoulder.

In the morning we were into the foothills of the Li Su mountains and the moorland farms, the little chicken farmers who sold their hens to Hong Kong, the charred fringe of the explosion area. Bodies were bloated in the black fields, ballooned into strange shapes of obesity, and on their chests sat the carrion crows of Myen in flea-scratching and hoarse caws. It was dreadful, and many of the people were sick and weeping.

The sun hissed and flamed in violet-rays of green and gold; the baked earth shimmered and stank; the water-holes and streams were dry, evaporated in the one searing five-second flame of the explosion. The people drooped and lagged.

"Move, move!" I cried, striding among them.

To delay now to rest meant death.

For the key to survival was now water, not rice. Thirst dominated the rumbling belly. Gasping, clinging to each other, the people stumbled on over the brittle grass of abandoned fields. Where a generation of China's youth had died, the blackened wheat of the first reaping lay in tangled skeins of blast under an oyster-coloured sky. Once all was fertile and lovely here, for I knew this land. Before the accident this place was gay with flashing paddies, red-roofed pagodas and chanting peasants. Now all was death as we passed the farms. The land wore an anxious hollow frown of hunger. Like dots of mortifying flesh around the edge of a wound, the dead were huddled in groups outside their shattered homes, the scaly crackling of their naked bodies telling of death by fire. Ancient ploughs raked at the sky in defiance of nuclear fission. Nothing moved in this dust-bowl of horror; neither bird, wind nor leaf. Tomb-like in the heat, Kwangtung north of Lo Wu was dead in the clutches of flame.

With darkness came wind. In the peaks of Li Su mist was swirling, barging and shouldering among the crags as if in haste to drown the dead earth. Seeing this, the people began to pray to ancient gods, which was despicable. They knelt on the pass with lighted joss-sticks in their hands, kowtowing as of old, shrieking their incantations, until I dragged them up

33

and hauled them on. With wind came rain, and it was precarious among the peaks. One slip meant death. I raced among them, warning them, threatening them with the edge and the pit-blackness of the five hundred feet drop to the plains. I cajoled, I begged them, but they only moaned and stumbled on, heedless of disaster. One scream, one death, and I should have to appear before the Party. No gold, says Chairman Mao, can buy a single peasant from a commune in China. The rain bucketed, it tub-washed, it flooded down the brimming tracks and culverts. It roared in foaming torrents off the ledges above us, cascaded down in baths of purifying water, and thundered over the precipices into the plains. Drenched, stained yellow with the bright mud of the crevices, the people laboured behind me in a shambling, numb follow-the-leader. Discipline was easier: they obeyed me without question, even the women, each seeking the comfort of servility in their mist of pain.

One, however, was alone and above this attitude. The giant peasant Yuen Sun Johnny walked two yards behind me all the way. Stripped to the waist he went, his body shining with sweat and rain, his manner indestructible. I remember that I had stopped the column on the crest of a rise and was reading my map when I heard the scream.

"What was that?"

The rain scuffled into us with a new fury. Tense, I listened.

"It was nothing," he said.

Later, they told me that the child Annoi, she of the bandaged knee, screamed twice when she fell.

"There it is again," I said.

"It is the wind," said Yuen Sun Johnny.

Such sounds are heard in the old Chung Mountains: the screams come from the tortured of the past, the legends say; a strange, eerie lute note, the plaintive symphony of the crags. The track, the pass is most difficult.

In centuries past this was the way of the invader and the merchant camel trains bearing the gold of the west and the silks of the east in trade. Along these tortuous ways have rumbled the caravans of the fidalgos, the hook-nosed aristocrats of Macau who brought sandalwood from Malacca in Port Malaya in exchange for the beautiful Japanese and Timorese slave-girls sold to the whore-houses of Hong Kong and Macau. Palanquins and sedans have carried the great and glorious here; under the lash of brutal traders have staggered the great negroes of Mozambique for the galleys of Japan.

"You know much of such things," said Yuen Sun Johnny.

In French I spoke to him then, also in English, even in the Peking dialect which he did not understand, and he was much impressed.

"Tell me, woman," he said, his hands together, for a Chinese peasant loves learning. This I told him:

That a fleet leaving Nagasaki in the seventeenth century discharged bar-silver through this place, bound for the palaces of Peking. Through these passionless rocks had been dragged the cannons of conquest born in the foundries of Manoel Bocarro; silken mantillas were worn along these tracks; the early martyrs, the Jesuits, carried Japanese screens. And while the gilt dome of Macau played the Angelus and raised its perfumed incense above heathen Chinese, so Lofu the Tiger pronounced the dreaded punishment of the *strappado*, which is a wrenching out of the limbs, in the name of God. Here, I told him, in this barbaric place was carried the treasure of the Ming emperors, the pearls and diamonds, the tapestries of Tientsin, the marvellous brocades of old Shanghai. Here the heresies of Solor and Cambodia were sounded on the thighbone trumpets of Tibertian virgins.

The child screamed again.

The people were pressed against the rock face, terrified. They had lit little sticks of incense in this new terror, and they would not burn in the rain. Some, braver than the rest, lay on their stomachs staring into the blackness below.

"What is it?" I hauled them aside.

35

"It is the child Annoi!"

"Another of the family Wen."

"Damn this family Wen," I said.

"She was walking near the edge; the wind took her, and she fell."

But I turned back, staring down, for the child was whimpering from the blackness below the precipice. I stared at Yuen Sun Johnny and he smiled back at me, saying:

"You are afraid of heights?"

The bile rose in my throat and I swallowed it down. The people shoved and jabbered with this new excitement. Tall in the crowd I saw the old elder of Hoon, and in his face I saw the scene of Hoon, the square: this, the one who called me Eurasian, the bastard of Sun Commune. I said:

"Is this your child?"

"By my first wife, her and the cripple boy."

"You are going down for her?"

"Woman, I beg of you. . . . Mei Kayling!"

I was terrified, and began to shiver. The shivering flew to my mouth and I covered it with my hands. Yuen Sun Johnny said:

"What is this to the new Red Guard? It is only five hundred feet."

"Who got a rope?"

"Red Guard is goin' down."

"Can't see the river below, you hear the river?"

The moon blazed in a rent of clouds, then pulled down skirts, bringing the pass to darkness. The wind moaned.

"Only got girdles."

"Tear up a coat?"

"*Whee-ah!* Off with the trousers."

"Tie up the legs!"

They shouted, they pushed in horse-play, all weariness gone. Belts and girdles were flung at my feet. Kneeling, men tore up jackets, knotting the seams in gasps of strength; the rope grew longer. Somebody shouted, "Make sure she don't part on the edge, or we got no Red Guard leader!"

36

"Over she goes!"

I knotted the make-shift rope around my waist. "Bring forward the Hoon elder, the man Wen!" I cried.

He came through the press of people, his face pale. I said:

"You first to hold the rope. One slip, and you lose your daughter."

As they dangled me into space the child began to scream in a sort of rhythmic scolding, at the delay.

A little wind blew in bitter intimacy around my thighs. Pebbles, dislodged by my clawing fingers, ran in icy trickles between my breasts. I looked up, seeing against a sudden brightness of the moon a circle of faces against the candle-stars. Bracing myself against the rock face, I reached down when they had sunk me twenty feet, and touched the face of Annoi, then screwed my body round the jutting crag that had broken her fall, and her back. The white bandage round her knee held me with rooted force.

"Annoi," I said, and she started at the sound of my voice.

"Annoi, it is me, Red Guard!" I gasped this, scrambling for support beside her. Faintly, from far below me, came the sound of the river.

Although her eyes were wide open they did not turn to me; then, to my astonishment, she reached out, feeling for me, gripped my arm, and smiled.

It was as if she were blind.

"Little Girl," I said, for this was her name, and held her.

A bubble of blood welled at the corner of her mouth and she sighed, then slipped easily into death.

"Oh no," I said, "it is not as easy as that. You are coming up, you are no use to me dead."

A voice bawled from above, not the voice of her father:

"Is the child alive?"

I knew then that if I said the child was dead they would leave me on the ledge to die with her.

"Alive and well," I shouted back, "pull me up!"

I laid the blood-soaked body of Annoi at the feet of her father, and went through their threats and curses back to the head of the column.

CHAPTER FOUR

Thrusting out of a night of blueness and cold, the sun rose at dawn with incinerating fire. Light hosed and sprayed into the flooded valley, now bright gold with running sun-splinters from the ancient oyster-beds of shattered mother-of-pearl.

The peasant Yuen Sun Johnny came to me and said, "This morning you will go to San Ho for the snakehead?"

"I go now, if I can keep these moving."

"I will keep them moving. Go."

I looked back at him. I did not like it, but he was all I had.

Hauling my rucksack tighter over my shoulders, I vaulted the berm and ran along the track to the village of San Ho three miles on down the plain. Here, the Party had told me, there would be a snakehead especially appointed to lead us through the wire of the Hong Kong border post; also a hundred and eighty catties of rice, bandages, even new clothes.

No mention had been made of a public execution.

The Great Light had withered San Ho. This, once beautiful, was a village that had been coffined by the slam of a lid. I walked slowly into a roasting-pot of human dead, taking the middle of the road with the smashed shanties crouched on either side, as if for a spring. Across the track the village buffaloes lay in balling putrescence, their drum-stick legs slanting skywards at rakish angles, for buffaloes die with frightening indignity. A child's head, shrunken by fire, regarded me with socketed eyes from the verge, and nearby, in grotesque attitudes, the villagers lay staring at the molten sun, hundreds upon hundreds, an incredible carnage by heat. I walked slowly, the skin of my scalp crawling with sensation. A rifle with a fixed bayonet lay across my path, and

38

automatically I stooped and picked it up, carrying it at the ready. I cursed the Party. It was enough to have to live under the threat of a trigger-happy America; unforgivable that such a holocaust should come through domestic negligence. Heads would roll. There would be a purge of the scientists that would leave its impact on China for a decade. Seeking the central aid post, I walked on. Burial parties had been at work here, but the dead were still profuse: heaped in doorways, lying in the fields where the heat had shrivelled them, they bore in their sightless faces the tragedy of my generation. These peasants of Kwangtung had been born into the bludgeoning of bad gentry and international squeeze: for the new order of the Communists their fathers had fought and died under the axes of the traitor Chiang Kai-shek. Now, in the very arms of the Cultural Revolution, they had been caught in the pincers of science and died by fire in a test-tube accident. No Party propaganda could explain this catastrophe, no high level speech even from the greatest love in China, Chairman Mao, could erase this blundering set-back. The West would bandy this failure before the noses of future generations.

It was then that I heard it, a distant galloping of feet.

By some strange trick of echo it came from every direction, and I turned in a circle, trying to identify its position. Louder, louder, like the hoof-beats of a chain-armour knight rushing from darkness, I heard it, then, identifying the sound, I swung to face it. Down the middle of the track a black dot was racing towards me, its feet drumming in the rhythmic pounding of a horse galloping. Nearer, nearer. I raised the rifle instinctively as the dog sprang, saw it sail towards me, forelegs spread, teeth bared. And I saw, too, in a flash of the sun, the bright steel of the bayonet thrust through its belly and out through its backbone, cutting off its shriek. I knelt in the road gripping the rifle with the dog writhing on the bayonet above me, its bright, hot blood gushing over my hands. Leaping away, I knelt in the dust of the road and watched the dog die in convulsive twitching. When it was dead I pulled out the bayonet and flung away the rifle. With the bayonet still in my hand, I turned on the road.

"You did him good, woman," said the man, and I swung to him.

He was a young Communist soldier, impossibly boyish in his ill-fitting uniform. Fear was restricting reply. I looked him up and down. His sudden appearance after the killing of the dog was unnerving.

"I am a Red Guard," I said.

It was supposed to impress him, but did not. The eternal quest for power between us and the Communist Youth League had no place in his profound adolescence.

I said, "What are you doing here?"

"Waiting for the central aid post."

"They haven't arrived?"

"They sent me forward from the Border Post three days back. I am still waiting."

I closed my eyes, and he said:

"You got people, Red Guard?"

"Eight hundred people."

"One party come through yesterday, he got twelve hundred; no aid post for him, neither. He hanged a snake-head other end of the village, and took them on."

"Did he say his name?"

The boy shrugged.

"Kwan To Lin?" I asked, eagerly.

"Didn't say his name."

"Tall man, handsome, dark?"

"This one put his nose up."

This sounded like Kwan.

"Why for he hang snakehead?" I spoke the old language to put him at ease.

"Took him three mile back to Kwangtung."

Yes, this was Kwan. I could have shouted his name with gladness.

"What time you bringing them down?" He glanced up at the mountain.

"It don't matter now, there being no aid post."

He came closer, watching me. "Where you taking them through?"

"Lok Ma Chau."

"Over the river?" His voice held faint derision. "The guards say you can walk over the bodies at Lok Ma Chau, for a flash flood come like '62 and the people drowned."

He said more but I did not hear him. I was thinking about Kwan. With blood on my hands and face, I was thinking about Kwan. The soldier said:

"And they got a thousand soldiers with black faces and long knives down the border at Lok Ma Chau."

"Ghurkas?"

"And another thousand Hong Kong police, an' they don't like Communists. The people are sitting on the Fanling hills waiting to rush the wire, but the guns are out. The yellow ox gangs are getting them through to Macau by junk, but you've got to have entry papers. The people just sit and cry." He looked at me. "You ever heard ten thousand people crying?"

I said indignantly, "The people will go in. Hong Kong belong to China!"

He opened his hands with an air of resignation. I shouted, "She belongs to China, and nobody is keeping the people out of Lok Ma Chau!"

He stirred the body of the dog with his boot. "Why don't you take them through Lo Wu?"

"Because I've got instructions."

"Everybody's got instructions. But you'll find worse than mad dogs in Lok Ma Chau."

It was the way he looked at me.

I left him and went back into the mountains.

As if in haste to purify San Ho of her ignominious dead, it began to rain.

This is the trouble with China: rain and drought come with total force.

Kwangtung, located in an abandoned bed of the Yellow

41

River, had once endured three hundred days of drought; two thousand people had died of hunger in this region; the roads were jammed with emigrating families begging and selling their children. And while this place dried into a dust-bowl the waters of flood were raging over neighbouring Kiangsi; hundreds were drowned, thousands of homes swept away in the torrent. As I climbed upwards I looked at the stricken sky, remembering the terrible East River floods of thirteen years ago. If they came now all my people might die.

Now the oceans fell, not rain, from vicious, flame-shot clouds. A million tons dropped instantly on Chung Mountains. In sudden, vivid light the sky was riven, and the water, rushing over the cementing action of drought, fell in tub-washes that bucketed over the scorched fields, gathered up the dead and piled them into the brimming irrigation canals of the dead communes. Giant gushes spewed from fissures in the mountains and poured headlong into the brimming plains. As if in recompense for the Great Light of the scientists that had murdered thousands, the rain baled up in the oceans of the sky and tipped on to Kwangtung a wave of roaring water that flew in bright red rivers to the mothering sea, sweeping up the dead like the refuse of autumn.

Guarded by Yuen Sun Johnny, a self-appointed leader in my absence, the people were crouched in the shelter of the rocks when I found them, more drowned than alive; bed-raggled puppets of misery, hair tangled, their peasant rags stained yellow with mountain soil. The old compradore Sung Po came to me then.

"Woman, I would speak with you."

"You stopped the column?"

"In the name of humanity, I and the big peasant, Yuen. You were gone two hours and the people were afraid; some sat on the pass and cried."

"I have been to San Ho, and there is no central aid post; something has gone wrong."

"There is no food?"

"There is water in abundance," I answered. "Tell them to drink."

He said, "It is not the hunger, they do not cry for that."

There was yet a dignity showing through the age; once this man was great. So great was he, so wealthy, that he owned two villages and possessed many bond-maids, with which to do as he pleased. The compradore of Suwen was well known in Peking. Sentenced to death by the army of Chiang Kai-shek, he was led to the village square, there to be publicly garrotted for profiteering out of the Nationalist Occupation, but Sung Po, the compradore of Suwen, did not die. He called, in his stead, a young coolie whose wife and three children were starving. And to this coolie Sung Po offered six hundred dollars to die in his place. To this the coolie agreed, and the money was paid to the wife. Sung Po took his place in the watching crowd, the coolie bent his head to the garrotting cord.

This is what China calls poverty.

Sung Po said now, "They thirst and hunger but they do not cry for that. Tomorrow they will reach Hong Kong. Many have relatives there, and they will lose face if they arrive dishevelled. It is essential that the peasant should be clean."

"I will see to this," I said.

Half a mile down the pass towards the plains I found a cave, and this was filled with foaming water. I sent a young girl messenger back to the people and they came in minutes, running with new fire down the slope to the bath, pulling their samfoo jackets over their heads, shaking out their hair. Young men and maidens, children, even the aged went hand-in-hand into the cave. For while there is morality in the New China there is no mock modesty. I watched them. Shafts of sunlight from the fissures in the roof made splendid play on their brown bodies. It could have been a scene from some primaeval play: here a mother plaiting the hair of her daughter, here a husband bathing his child, and the young ones, girls and boys, splashing in the coldness, shrieking, flinging water in sprays of diamond light. As a hundred came out so a hundred went in, and some made smiles of warmth as they passed me. Later, because I was not of them, I went to a smaller pool farther down the track and there took off my uniform. The sun was setting. Kwangtung was incredibly beautiful in the rain. My hair, tied tightly under my cap, was drenched. I took out the strings and pulled it over my shoulders and the old dye that lay at the roots ran down my body in little streams of black. Distantly, I heard the clamour of the people; hands outstretched for balance I waded into the pool, and turned to the sound of a footstep.

Yuen Sun Johnny was standing in the cave entrance, and he was as naked as I.

His eyes drifted over me in calm assessment.

"What you doing here?" I said.

"Who is to know, woman?"

He grinned stupidly, his vulgar strength skidding over the yards between us. There was about him an obscene beauty, the image of the ancient landowner from whom he came: in him was the right to own by lust. Even twenty years back he would have done the same. And the bond-maid he demanded would have wept: with her arms crossed on her breast she would have wailed before the watching men.

Strangely, I was trembling, but not with cold.

One of the greatest dangers to a system is the frailty of humans when the greatest strength is needed.

"Back where you came from," I said, and waded towards him, "or I come from here and tip you over the edge."

After he had gone I covered my face with my hair.

CHAPTER FIVE

At dawn Yuen Sun Johnny came to me again. I pulled my blanket aside and rose, facing him.

"There are eighteen people missing," he said.

"Do not be stupid!"

44

"Eighteen. I counted once, Sung Po twice."

"They have gone back down the pass," I said, buttoning my tunic.

"They have not. I have sent two young ones five miles back, and they saw nobody. Besides, they are afraid to travel alone in the mountains."

Sung Po came running then, crying. "Some have been seen, Yuen. They go over the top."

"Where?"

He pointed into the valley. In the first faint light of dawn I saw three bodies on the rock below.

"Three might have fallen, but not eighteen." I pushed him aside and ran down the pass to where a group of women were weeping and wringing their hands. One cried, "Missus, my son fell, also my sister's child, aged fifteen."

"In the night they fell!"

"Not a sound we heard."

I asked, "Did they jump?"

"You remember Che Min, the harvester of Revival Commune?" cried another.

They nodded assent, staring down at the three bodies twisted in grotesque attitudes of mutilation.

"He fell about midnight, for I heard him cry out."

I demanded, "What was he doing roaming about in darkness?"

"Went to ease his leg."

I turned to Yuen Sun Johnny. "Come with me, we are going down."

We went the long way down the track, turning east on the plains just before the sun rose with her bucket of fire, and this she stuffed up the chimney of the day and stoked it red. The heat blazed, the outcrop rocks reflected blinding light.

The harvester Che Min we found first; he had fallen over two hundred feet yet his face was unmarked, smooth and pale in death. His sightless eyes stared straight into the sun, strangely opaque, the pupils shrunken.

"Him blind," said Yuen Sun Johnny.

We found another, the child of Jeck Nin, the brigade leader of Old Suwen, a girl. She had fallen late, her hands and face being warm. This one also, as blind as night.

I said, "This is the blindness of the Great Light. It comes instantly, like the shut of a curtain."

Yuen said: "These peasants are either from Hoon or down the road to Myen. All who were in the fields would have seen the Light come, for it was the first reaping."

"We move them quick now," I replied. "No more go blind before we reach Hong Kong." I turned to him. "Where were you when the Light came?"

"In the stack-yard, baling up. I saw it through the window."

I stared at him and he grinned back, adding, "Take more than that to blind Yuen Sun Johnny."

"You saw it also? Why did you not say?"

"You did not ask me."

"Where did it blaze? From north of Canton?"

"From the east, in the mountains."

I gripped his arm, turning him. "You are sure of this, quite sure?"

"It blazed in the mountains."

On the way to the hamlet of Lu-Sun the people faltered; this was partly because I would not stop to bury their dead. When they would not move I ran among them calling them terrible names, saying that they were behaving like Americans, the soft-bellied people. This only served to infuriate them. Earlier there had been a terrible sign, and the old superstitions had come upon them; death, they said, was now inevitable. We had seen an ancient peasant sitting on the track in fluttering rags, one skeleton arm outstretched, pointing the way. On the arm perched a carrion crow; another was upon his head. This was terrifying, for we demand dignity in death. Many people cried; children screamed against their mothers.

Now they shielded their bodies against kicks and blows and sat rocking themselves and moaning.

The genius of Yuen Sun Johnny did not all lie below the waist. He idly told them that it was but a few days to the custom of Ching Ming, which is a sweeping clean of the graves of ancestors, and many had ancestors in Hong Kong. Their duty was clear, and some rose, shambling behind him. Others followed like sheep, the rest dared not die alone. The order of march was now this. I was leading. Behind me came Yuen and Sung Po. After them came the aged, the young helping them, then the middle-aged. Last of all walked the blind. The blind, and there were now eleven of them, were knotted together with coat-seams, hands pawing the air, like a funeral train. In this manner, in the cooling sunset, we reached Lu-Sun.

This was the blackened edge of the explosion, a gigantic cemetery of unburied dead which shimmered and stank in the sunset gold. Here groups of blind peasants wandered, wailing to the agony of their burns. Children ran delirious with pain, babies shrieked from scorched huts. About the shattered compounds of the commune the plantations lay in shrivelled desolation. I marched on, pitiless, looking neither left nor right while the villagers tore at my hands, imploring help.

Yuen cried, "You know where the medical post is?"

"There was none in San Ho," I replied.

"And there might be one here, in Lun-Sun?"

"If there is one these people would have found it." I snatched at a vagrant boy, one arm hanging useless by his side, and cried:

"You see first-aid place come?"

He screwed up his face to the pain of his blistered body and rolled his eyes at the sky. I shouted, "Answer me! Why for you not go see man doctor?"

The child did not reply. I said, "It is the dialect, he is not from these parts."

"It is his pain," said an old crone. "His tongue is dry in his throat."

"You know this village?" I asked her.

"Every lane and plough. Each oxen I know by name, the

grain on every bough. Tell Peking, who sent us the Big Light, to send us white doctors from the land of Hong Kong, and we shall live again."

"Look!" whispered Yuen Sun Johnny.

It was a migration from the suburbs of Canton. Behind a rolling billow of dust they came, a thousand people blinded. Nearer, nearer, and I halted my column. The dust settled around the flanks of the army and I saw it clearly: a population of the blind, hands outstretched, fingers gripping shoulders. They hung on trailing ropes, they straggled hand in hand, many falling, to lie still while the army passed over them. They wheeled, all direction lost, spilling in their wake the weakest, the young and old. And at their head, taking them in a wide curve back into China, walked a Hong Kong snakehead, his newspaper cap, signal of his authority, at a jaunty angle on his head.

"He is taking them north?" said Yuen.

This was the way of the snakeheads of Hong Kong. They would receive money from the emigrants to lead them over the border, then take bribes from the border post guards to lead their columns back into China. A cheap compass can hang the most cunning snakehead, but these people of Canton had gone blind on the march.

"Take him?" said Yuen.

"Let him hang himself," I said.

He turned then, this snakehead, and seeing us he shouted that we should join his column which was going into Hong Kong. My people gathered about me, staring.

I said, "Take two men and bring me the snakehead."

"I get this one alone," said Sung Po, coming up.

"And turn those people to the rear of our column, Yuen Sun Johnny. The blind with the blind, the young with the young who are not blind."

"That is madness," he said. "You expect to take two thousand people through the wire?"

"First bring me the snakehead."

The people formed a circle about me when they brought

48

the snakehead in. And he went on his knees before me, hands begging, bright saliva dribbling from his mouth. I said:

"Where you from?"

Terror was in him. He recognised the uniform of the Red Guard.

"From Hong Kong, missy."

"And you are being paid by these people to lead them over the border?"

He nodded violently, smelling death.

"Tell me," I continued, "does Hong Kong lie north or south of Lu-Sun?"

"South, missy!"

"Yet you lead the people north?"

The people gathered about him, a closer knot to tie him, and he stared about him in shivers and said, gasping, "First I take them north because of the road blocks, then I take them south. Every inch, I know the way. Yesterday I take a column through."

"From Canton?"

"From Fu Tin, Route Seven, the leader Kwan To Lin."

I raised my head to a strange and urgent joy.

"You led them through?"

"In the way their leader said. And two days back I brought in another and the leader was Ku Ata, a Japanese."

"By which route?"

"Over the paddy bridge and through the Tientsin cabbages."

"Which is the safest route tomorrow?"

He replied, with growing confidence, "There is a guard, a man of Shansi, who knows a hole in the wire six miles south as the crow goes. Five hundred dollars each it will cost, him and his mate demand this. But there are no black-faced soldiers there or Hong Kong police."

"Dogs?"

"None."

"They use this money to bribe the guards away?"

He nodded, erect now, with confidence.

49

I turned to Yuen Sun Johnny. "Hang him," I said.

Incredulity struck the snakehead's face and he slowly sank to his knees, reaching for my legs.

"Hang him," I said, "he is useless to China."

He shrieked once as they dragged him through the ranks of villagers, his boots beating dust from the flinted road. I watched while they pinned him: the young men knelt in urgent haste, tearing up seams. He did not cry again. Working beneath a tree they hoisted him high. He was still swinging as I got the people away.

In darkness I led the people down the track of the Shamchun River, the border fence between Hong Kong and China. I should have turned west for Lok Ma Chau but the black-faced soldiers were there, the young sentry said, so I turned south for Fanling. One thousand dollars I had for bribes; these I would give to the man of Shansi, the guard who knew the hole in the fence. If I had to fight I would fight, but it was smoother to bribe. The river was roaring in flood, guard dogs bayed at the moon as I took them down the north bank; from the darkness came the tinkle of bayonets and the gutteral whispers of men. When I reached the Shansi hole I stopped the column and sent for Yuen Sun Johnny.

"This is the hole in the wire," I said.

With a strange, new arrogance he replied, "How do you know this?"

"Because I am the leader." I gave him the thousand dollars. "This is a part cleared of the Hong Kong police. On the other side of the bridge you will find a Shansi snakehead, and his mate. Bribe them with this, then return, and I will bring the people through."

He said, fingering the money, "I could think of better places for this than in the pockets of snakeheads."

"Go," I commanded.

I watched him cross the bridge, then went back to the people; the first I met was Sung Po.

"So you sent Yuen with a thousand dollars?"

"It is cheap at the price," I answered. "Two thousand people at fifty cents a head, I am not having bloodshed."

"It is the last thing the big peasant wants," said Sung Po, "armed with a thousand dollars."

The people flocked down to the river bank and there knelt, scooping up handfuls of water and splashing it into their faces, bathing their eyes.

At midnight, an hour after Yuen Sun Johnny had left us, Sung Po came to me again, his face white with anger.

"Yuen has not returned?" he demanded.

"No," I said.

"And did you expect it? He is from the landlord class, the blood smiles through. He has been seen, you know."

"By whom?"

He called a child and she stood before me, one finger in her mouth, aged seven.

I knelt to her. "What is your name, girl?"

"Su Su."

Sung Po wailed at the sky; a thousand dollars lost, which might have been his.

I said, "Su, Su, they tell me you have seen the big peasant, Yuen Sun Johnny?"

She nodded; there was a fine arrogance about her also. "He called to me on the bridge, and I went."

"Did he speak to you?"

"He spoke to me. He said, 'Tell the white bitch that if she wants her thousand dollars to come to the Shansi man and beg for it.'"

I rose before her. "Excellent. Now go back to your mother."

Sung Po cried harshly, "Now are you satisfied?"

"Yuen Sun Johnny," I said, "will be satisfied long before me."

First I changed into peasant clothes, then I went down-river and over the bridge. Against the silver sheen of racing water three men were squatting: one was a Shansi giant, the second was his mate, a pygmy, the third was Yuen.

I said, coming up to them, "I seek a man called Yuen Sun Johnny."

This perturbed them and they chattered together, wondering where the hell such a man might be at that time of night and how fortunate he was to be wanted by a woman with such beauty.

"She has white hair," said Yuen. "Under her cap she has white hair that reaches to her shoulders, and there are good things under that samfoo worth squeezing, for I have seen them."

This made them shout with laughter, the little one rolling about. I said to Yuen, "If you see this man tell him this for me. Because he has stolen money belonging to the people, China will see that he dies."

The snakehead rose to his full height, a giant Huhehot from the big country, and said, double bass, "You have a witness that he stole this money?"

Next the pygmy climbed up. "Before a man is punished he must first be proved guilty, Red Guard. That is the law of Peking."

"And before you prove him guilty you first must catch him," this from Yuen Sun Johnny, grinning up.

"You could flay him alive," said the Huhehot, "but this will not get your two thousand people through this wire. This takes money to bribe the guards."

"How much?" I asked.

"One thousand dollars. See our position. What is the normal price of entry into the paradise of Hong Kong? Ten dollars a head? All we ask is fifty cents a head, is this unreasonable?"

"I have paid you the money," I replied, but he went on:

"There are bribes to pay at the border post, bribes to pay at Fanling and behind it, immigration officials to pay, documents to purchase."

"I have no more money."

"But other assets, such as women?"

"None to sell."

He opened his hands to me. "Then how will you get in?"

"I will rush the wire."

This caused tremendous consternation. They pushed and barged each other, then the Huhehot recovered.

"And land in Hong Kong with a thousand people less? The machine-guns are out. What would they say to that in Peking?"

I said, turning away, "You sent for me, tell me what you want of me."

Huhehot said, smiling, "You have a whiteness, and that is better than money. You are right, Yuen, she is a white beauty." Reaching out, he smoothed my hair from my face. The others came closer; I did not move.

"It do seem a pity."

"First time I looked on a white Cantonese."

"Tried her once before," said Yuen, "but she seemed reluctant."

They circled me. The Huhehot reached out and un-buttoned my collar, Pygmy swept off my cap and pulled down my hair; they giggled and pushed each other, the haystack fornication; manhood is at its worst when hunting in the mass. I recall thinking that, somewhere beyond the blaze of distant Hong Kong, Kwan would be waiting for me. It was an agreeable bargain, providing they kept their word.

I said, "I am not reluctant, if you let the people pass."

They knelt at my feet in new excitement, plucked grass and measured three blades. Yuen held them in his fist and the others drew; Huhehot drew the longest. Rising, he waved the others away and unhooked his belt.

"You had a man before, white girl?"

"Yes."

"Then this will come as no surprise. Down, woman, be obedient."

I was worried about the people. Only Sung Po was left to them. I said: "You will not kill me afterwards?"

He was trembling.

"Not if you please me."

The stars were green and gold with the threat of dawn, the sky flaring with puff-adder clouds, the edges streaming silver and tinged with a strange, rosy light. I thought: when I get clear of this man and his stupid gasps I will take the people in. I will take them in and head them west, not to Fanling where the English soldiers would be astride the road but to San Tin, the ancient city. Through San Tin and on to Yuen Long, the great new town where an army could hide. I would rest them there for the day, mixing with the Hong Kong population; the blind I would hide, the young ones I would send to forage food. And when night fell, in this same darkness made by the man of Huhehot, I would gather them again and march them pitilessly across the forests of the Tai Tam reservoir, the old Japanese attack route when they invaded Kowloon. Here, with water, they could again clean themselves before the last haul into the attics of the city. The man of Huhehot grunted above me, his head swept over the stars. I lay, gripping my hands.

"I am next," said Pygmy.

"Please," I said, "do not kiss my face."

To him I was a torment only, he being half a man.

"Mei Kayling," said Yuen Sun Johnny, "I am the last."

I opened my eyes, tuning my brain to the knowledge of him; listening to the wind, the staccato roaring of the river; getting the sense of every moment in time. I looked to the left, seeing nothing but the waving bank of the river; I looked to the right into the pulsating blaze of Hong Kong city. We were alone, I and Yuen Sun Johnny. My brain was alive, his was dead with pleasure.

At the best of times the sleek glide of a knife can be a surprise. At a time like this it can be disconcerting. His eyes opened wide in profound disbelief as I first put my left hand over his mouth, then, with my right hand, pushed the blade upwards. He sighed, put his cheek against mine, and died. Horizontally they are all at some disadvantage. Heaving him away, I knelt in the wet grass and took from his pockets the thousand dollars.

First I went down to the river to wash, then I went to the Huhehot.

"A receipt for this money, please," I said.

He stared down at me. "But the man Yuen . . .?"

"The man Yuen has changed his mind."

With the pygmy walking between us, we went through the wire to the guards. The Huhehot paid them money and I stood by as they packed and locked the machine-gun. Sung Po led the people through the wire into Hong Kong at three-thirty-six exactly. Actually, it was eighteen minutes later than in my written instructions. The delay, I reflected, would be difficult to explain.

There was little elegance in it: mistakes had been made and people had paid for them, including me. Kwan would never have got himself into such an awkward position; but it is given to few of us to attain the brilliance of Kwan.

As I went through the wire, the last to leave China, I called to the man of Huhehot:

"It is not goodbye. One day you and I will meet again."

He actually bowed, so did the pygmy, being delighted at the possibility.

CHAPTER SIX

Kwangtung was emptying its millions into the New Territories of Hong Kong, whole villages travelling in packs with their bedding and chattels bouncing on their shoulder-poles, coolie-fashion. They came with their young and aged, their babies on their backs; they came with their ancestors whose polished, perfumed bones were neatly packed in the great stone jars, feet at the bottom, skulls on top. Across the border posts at Lo Wu and Shan Tsu they came, paying their bribes to the Hong Kong police; down the dusty roads of Fanling and Yuen Long they flooded, an army of the blind, a plague of mouths, eating dry the larders and scavenging in the barns, their belligerence growing with desperation and hunger. On Bird Hill and Cloud Hill they lay exhausted and pocked the dull, forbidding country with their night-can fires. The fishing junks of the yellow ox-gangs were jammed to the gunwales; many capsized, and successive tides swarmed in the dishevelled dead over the beaches from Repulse Bay to Shek-O. Macau bulged at the seams as the black flood of human misery fought down the roads to the Barrier Gate. Many forded the river at Lok Ma Chau and even built rafts to cross Tolo Harbour, but the big winds came and swept them out into the China Run with tattered sails, to die. Thousands more died in ways that were not recorded; some by their own kind when money could not be extorted. Many died, too, in the mountains of China, led back there by the atrocious snakeheads. From Tai Kim to Ta Ku the snakeheads dangled on trees, summary justice by the village elders.

Because we were early out of Kwangtung we struck the villages first, and my young men looted and thieved like the others. To the east of San Hing there stood a rice barn, and we ate our way through one end and out the other, like starving ants. And from the flanks of the invading columns the people fell out and lay in scores at the roadside. Starving wonk dogs, the scavengers of China, banded together in the alleys of Yuen Long and ran in yelping packs for the Fanling hills. The pimps and procurers of festering Hong Kong came from their holes and snatched the people in: men for the sweated labour of the building sites, the children for the exploitation of the factories, the women for service to prostitution and the bars. British soldiers were on the streets of Victoria, machine-guns at the ready, and past them flooded the refuse of Kwangtung, a tattered, bandaged army of test-tube defeat. Long-shuttered windows opened to snatch a family here and there, two to a bed-cage, twenty to a room; stinks rose on the fetid air as the Wanchai poor opened its doors. And still the black tide flooded in, cramming the hospitals, spreading out its blankets in the alleys where ragged children danced to the agony of hunger and teen-age girls sold themselves in doorways for handfuls of rice. And despite the holocaust the bars were full; foreign sailors brawled and strutted through the tinsel establishments in their nightly gollop of beer and vice.

It began to rain as I went down Wanchai, softly at first, then beating in torrents off the fruit-stalls. With rain running out of my boots I stood at the entrance of Spring Garden Lane. I recognised the old house instantly, the place where I was born. Up a swaying staircase I went, and knocked on a door. Below me came the soprano shriek of women and the hoarse booms of men.

"Come in," Old Man said.

"Mei Kayling?" he asked. His accent was Tan-gar, which is of the Boat People of the Yellow River.

"I am Mei Kayling," I replied.

"You are late."

It was an excellent start. I travel over a thousand miles, I bring two thousand people in, and he tells me I am late. I said, slamming the door behind me:

"I am precisely on time. I waited outside two minutes to ensure it."

"But yesterday . . .!"

"It's time they changed you," I said, "You've got the date wrong."

He smiled imperceptibly, dropped a hook-bolt over the door and turned up the wick of a lamp. "It is the rain, Kayling," he said. "The rain gets into the head; it is better when one is young." The lamp flared and I saw his face clearly; old enough for embalmed dead, this one, yet with features of moving dignity, befitting the best espionage agent in China. He said:

"Sit, woman, sit."

"I am soaked. It is more comfortable to stand. You have seen Kwan To Lin?"

"I have orders to receive you, no other."

57

"Is he not due to report here also?"

"If he is I have no news of it. You brought the people in?"

"I brought in two thousand."

"You were not followed?" he asked.

"If I was I saw no sign of it. It is marvellous security to come in with two thousand."

He said, "Will you kindly remove your cap?"

I did so and he came closer; examining me in the poor light. "You have papers?"

I said, "You will have to take me on face value until you see Kwan. I have no papers. They are coming within a day by special messenger."

"Good." He rubbed his bony hands together, his straggled grey beard munching like a goat's. "Now you would like to eat? A bath, clean clothes?"

"Is this possible?"

He was of the old school, the school of dignity and good manners, of the embellished phrases and dreadful over-statement, but they still knew how to die.

"Anything is possible. For one who serves the people, the people will serve."

There was a bed near a window and I stood beside it, looking through the slit of the curtains into the Wanchai street. The gutter-spouts were pelting, the drowning tarmac was flying in sheets to the sea. Behind me Old Man was carrying in pails of steaming water, and these he poured into a hip bath, declining help with dignified restraint. When this was ready, he said:

"You will take this bath while I prepare the meal?"

"Of course." I began to remove my clothes.

"I am unfortunately beyond the charms of women, but I will leave the room, if you wish."

"It is of no importance."

While I bathed he fried giant prawns and boiled rice on an oil stove, taking not the slightest interest in me. The Party, I reflected, covers most contingencies, for the bed was surely made for two. From under its pillow he brought white

58

samfoo trousers and a jacket heavily stained with crimson flowers, and these he laid on a chair, together with a towel. As I got out of the bath, he said:

"Your hair is, as they said, very beautiful." He examined the bath water for stain, found none, and grinned his widest in reassurance.

"I am ashamed of this hair," I replied.

He began to lay the little table, throwing rice-china bowls upon it, laying out spoons and chop-sticks. "Yet one day it will serve you. Do not criticise its colour, examine only its strength. One day, in this game, it might lower you from a window."

"You will eat with me, Old Man?"

"Of course. Though I saw you in the bath the belly, to me, is the sole delight."

The people thronged along the pavement below us with a new thunder, vociferous in their hunger; the rain swept the window in windy gushes. Old Man ate with noisy relish, snapping at the chop-sticks like a dog at flies. He said:

"Once, in conversation with scholars, I read, 'There came a man from the tall country and he was fair: he mated with a woman of the East, and she was dark. The child of the mating was bright in the eyes, with fair complexion and white hair — the coming of a blackbird and white dove loving, an albino.'"

"I am not albino," I said.

He shrugged. "The Party makes occasional mistakes. The Hundred Flowers speech, for instance, was a mistake, in my opinion, if only because it gave the west the opportunity to deride its sincerity and shriek untruths. But the selection of one like you for a task like this is really quite excellent."

"The task is finished, in my belief," I said.

"The task is not yet begun, child. You were born in this house, I understand?"

"On the roof." I raised my eyes upward.

"It is the way one ends, not the way one is born."

I said, "My mother lived here once. She had a daughter,

59

my sister Chieh, by a Tan-gar fisherman, then he was drowned at sea. On the roof she lived in poverty. Then one day an English sailor came to Hong Kong. Coming ashore from one of the big cargo bummers he went into a bar, got drunk, fought another sailor, was pursued by many other sailors, with batons and strange hats, and ran up the stairs to this roof. My mother sheltered him. Later, still drunk, he went out and bought chow-fan and dried fish, and these he fed to my mother, for Chieh was at her breast, and she was starving. Later, he made love to my sister Chieh in coos and bubbles, as sailors make love to babies. Later still he made love to my mother, and she brought forth me."

"There have been worse beginnings." Old Man sucked his teeth with joyful relish.

"But not so many." I leaned my chin in my cupped hands and stared through the curtains. "For two years we lived in Hong Kong, and for some strange reason my parents married. Apparently my father adored me, for I was in his image. He was going to take my mother and me to England, and for this purpose he obtained passports, but he would not bring Chieh, my half-sister; she was to be left behind. A week before we were due to leave, my father died."

"And then?"

"We grew poor. My mother took us to Macau, where Chieh and I worked in the firecracker factory up at Barra. When I was ten years old she took us into China, to the village of Hoon."

"So you have known poverty also. This is good."

I said, "It is good for those who watch, not for those who endure it. You see this hand?" I held up my left hand. "This hand, in Macau, kept us from starvation. With my right hand I chopped wood, fetched and carried, cooked at the fire, grubbed in bins for food."

"But your left hand was the bread-winner, eh?" He grinned, showing broken teeth. I said:

"This left hand was never allowed to become too cold or too hot: at night my mother wrapped it in muslin, and in the morning rubbed in oils; it was a most beautiful hand, soft as lotus blossom."

"Beautiful, beautiful!" His goat beard waggled on his pruney chin.

I got up, walking about. "Comparing one hand with the other you would have been astonished." I held my hands towards him. "See now, the difference! The right is strong and sinewy, say for a knife; the left is as soft as a chicken's breast. This left hand could pick the back-pocket of an American sailor without his giving a wink!"

"This, of course, is art!" Old Man was delighted, rocking his stomach, guffawing to bring down plaster. I continued:

"But one day in Macau, down the *Rua da Felicidade*, I was nearly caught. I had my beautiful left hand deep in the trousers of a big black Mozambique when he tripped and fell, and there we were rolling about, trying to get free. I lost him and ran home, pursued by black Mozambiques and half the guard of the *comissário*, then hid in Camoens Gardens. They did not catch me."

"For a Red Guard Second Class that is an enormous tale!" Old Man slapped his thigh with gusto. "And then?" He peered, joyfully.

"This was a great set-back to my career. It meant that I could no longer pick pockets. I should have to work full time in the firecracker factory and end like Patti Rea, who had no eyes or hands, or the family Solvari, the black Ports who coughed themselves to death."

"So you left Macau?"

"We left Macau and travelled to Hoon, in China." I spread my hands. "And there, for you, the story ends?" I watched him closely.

"There, for me, the story just begins," he said, listening to footsteps on the stairs. "When that door opens we turn another page."

He rose to his feet.

"Come in, Pak Lin Ho," he said.

A woman entered the little room; there was about her a faded beauty. Life might have taken a fist to her face and body, but nothing could diminish her dignity. At first sight she held an extraordinary resemblance to my dead mother.

Old Man bowed, closing the door behind her.

"Pak Lin Ho, your mother," he said to me.

I was not surprised. "You have done well," I replied. "You have even achieved a physical likeness — but I cannot think why."

"Mei Kayling?" The woman bowed slightly.

Old Man said, "Examine her well, Kayling. Your life may depend on it."

The woman said, "The girl must be tired; this would be best done tomorrow."

"The negro comes tomorrow," replied Old Man. "This must be done tonight." He sat on the bed and began to fill a little silver pipe.

"Negro?" I asked.

Old Man waved me down. "Later, later. She is your mother. Examine her."

"Please proceed," said Pak Lin Ho.

I said, "Tell me, how long did you live here?"

The woman answered, "Until you were about two years old."

I motioned her to a chair. "Please sit down. Tell me, why did you leave?"

She shrugged, a most excellent actress. I often wondered where they got these people from: many, I knew, came from the State Academy, but the Politburo had recently appointed a director of a special branch of dramatic art. Her very calmness suddenly infuriated me, and I swung to Old Man.

"She knows her part, when do I know mine?"

"In my good time." He lit the pipe in a flare of match and smoke, ignoring my anger. "Please continue."

The woman was watching me, and I said, more calmly, "You were going to tell me why you left Hong Kong?"

"Because your father died. Hong Kong was bad for me. I

lost my first husband here; there was no point in staying."

"My father was British," I said. "Why did you not seek help from the British Government?"

"Because I committed the sin of being Chinese."

"Where did you take me?"

"To Macau."

"And my half-sister Chieh?"

"She came also. She was four years old. You were only two, and most of the time had to be carried, I remember."

"How long did we live in Macau?"

"Until you were aged sixteen, then we returned here."

"And my sister, Chieh?"

"She died in Macau at the age of seven."

I put my hands to my head. "It is going to take some remembering, all this."

The woman said, "I have had to remember it, every word, and so will you."

Old Man interjected, "Come now, do not haggle."

Lin Ho's face was strained. The trouble with espionage is that it is the effort of a team. I might be satisfying myself as to her ability to impersonate my mother, but she also demanded the satisfaction that I was a reasonably intelligent daughter. I said:

"And when I was sixteen you renewed my passport in my own name. Why did you do this?"

"Times were better in Macau. I saved money. Your European appearance determined me to take you to England."

"But you did not do this?"

"No. I obtained an excellent post here at Daimaru's. Later I worked at Sun Ya, as a waitress."

"And I?"

She said wearily, "Hong Kong creates problems for the young. You were no exception. First you worked in a carpet factory, later in a dance hall. . . ." She turned to Old Man, saying icily, "Why was she not instructed in all this?"

He puffed his pipe. "Because I am a foreign agent. I am

not responsible for the shortcomings of the Central Espionage – talk to Kwan To Lin."

"Where do I work now?" I asked.

"In the Ho Tai bar, in Jaffe Street. At this bar you earn two hundred dollars a month plus anything you can get from men who buy you out."

"And where do I live?"

"Where you are standing now. We lived together, first on the roof; later, your father rented this floor in his name, which was Warren. Through the years your real mother sub-let it, but I have the rent books, everything is in perfect order."

I said, "I do not like all this. I have had no notice of it. I have no time to assimilate it. I demand to see Kwan To Lin."

Old Man said wearily, "Woman, we are fulfilling the instructions of Kwan To Lin; now do not annoy us with silly tantrums."

"It is confusing, and I do not like it, I say. If I have my own plan of movement and identity it would be much safer."

"If you have your own plan of movement and identity you have nobody in the world who can corroborate it."

I got up. "I demand to see Kwan. I demand to know the project and what is required of me before I lend myself to this stupid fiction."

"You have spent your time in China," said Lin Ho. "It is this fact that we are trying to obliterate." She turned to Old Man with deliberate boredom. "It is a fiction that Kwan considers her capable of this; take my advice and send her back to Hoon."

I was desperately tired. They might have given me a sleep. They had not seen the holocaust of San Ho or the charred craters of Hoon. It seemed to me that they were weaving an aura of romance and artifice into a situation of tragedy and terror; a superficiality of officialdom that mocked the misery of the scurrying refugees on the packed streets below us. I looked through the curtains, ignoring Old Man and the woman. In the garish neon signs of Wanchai I saw khaki-clad Hong Kong policemen standing with batons at the ready, while the refugees, many badly burned, walked in double file between them, their arms clear of their sides to escape the agony of friction. It was like the evacuation of the embers of a bonfire, the roasted ants escaping. Turning from the window, I said, more gently:

"Please continue, Lin Ho."

"The questions are yours, Kayling. I am here to answer."

"Be additionally comforted," said Old Man. "It is difficult for everybody, including me. But it is most difficult of all for Lin Ho. Hers is the biggest responsibility if ever you come to American interrogation, which, believe me, is not the softest in the world. Tomorrow I will give you the project in detail, tonight you will practise this new relationship. Like you, Lin Ho has her instructions. If caught she will corroborate every detail of your life; if she fails you will know an undying consolation. The pills she has with her are a cyanide base; they work in fifteen seconds."

The woman said, "Now we will have your questions again. We will have them slowly, in some semblance of order, one by one, and we will have them without heat and certainly without emotion."

Later, they let me go to bed. They sat by the window, these two, talking in whispers, so that I could sleep, but I did not sleep. I lay there reliving the march from Hoon; also, there was a pain in me because of the man of Huhehot. Later, I fell into a shuddering, sweating drowse, dreaming of Kwan. But in the morning, with sunlight streaming through the window, the pain was gone and I awoke refreshed to the challenge of the day.

I was wondering about the negro.

CHAPTER SEVEN

The room was empty when I awoke, but the woman Lin Ho had been active while I slept: laid over a chair was a sleek, silver cheongsam, silk stockings, and all the briefs and brassières of the western aids to sex-titillation. On a little chest of drawers she had put the paint and mascara of the harlot. I washed and dressed and powdered and painted. A very different Mei Kayling stood on stilt-heeled shoes like a hobbled donkey. There is a finality and oblivion in blind acceptance. If one has to wear the personality of the prostitute, one might as well look the part. The effect, however, was a little surprising. Though morally it was a change for the worse, constitutionally it was for the better. The dress, I reflected, was extremely pretty.

Old Man came in while I was considering this. He said:

"The westerners have a word for this. I believe they call it ravishing. There is perfume on the table, she told me. It is worn behind the ears."

I had never before used perfume; the smell was enchanting, like a Shansi poppy field in summer.

"Persist in these trifles and you will actually become feminine," he said. "A rare combination, Kayling, perfume and karate."

I said, "I do not like her."

"Lin Ho? Guard these likes and dislikes: they impede, deter and destroy. She is a most efficient woman — university degree, expert in electronics, what more ability do you need?"

I did not speak. I was still wondering about the negro. No doubt Old Man would explain this, in his own time. I plied the mascara brush, watching him in the mirror. He said, "The newspapers are giving the results of hospital tests upon the injured. They are remarkable. Even those within a quarter of a mile from the hypocentre of the explosion suffered only burns and blindness. There is absolutely no vomiting or epilation."

"Epilation?"

"A falling out of the hair. And almost no petechiæ, the small haemorrhages under the skin, and no gastro-intestinal symptoms like those they found in Hiroshima."

"The bomb was clean?"

66

"If such a thing exists. It is known that in the closed area north-east of Canton certain advanced nuclear experiments were being carried out, but it is difficult to believe that we were as advanced as that."

"All this is in the Hong Kong papers?"

"A little is my own information. The flash, however, was brighter than Nagasaki and Hiroshima put together. An aircraft landing at Kai Tak reported seeing it when three hundred miles away. I saw a man walking in Queen's Road East; a little child was leading him. The man's nose and ears were melted away, and he was blind. Upon his head was a ring of hair where his coolie cap had been, yet he was alive."

"He was dead," I said, putting on lipstick.

Behind me he fired the kettle for tea. Tea was Old Man's passion; nuclear retaliation, espionage, all waited until Old Man had drunk his tea. I said:

"And what about the negro you mentioned?"

"Ah yes, he will be here tonight."

"Would it be too much to explain why he comes and what I am going to do with him?"

Old Man's cherished possession was surely a sense of the dramatic. With slow emphasis he said, "Two days before the Kwangtung disaster there were in the Hong Kong naval base one destroyer, two frigates and three minesweepers, also a white survey ship that comes into Tamar from time to time — all British. In the harbour flow there were an American aircraft carrier and four destroyers, also a submarine which was berthed within the base. It is my task to keep checks on these comings and goings; much of espionage is absolute routine, as you know. Vigilance is tightened when the Americans bring in a nuclear-powered carrier, but the day-to-day activity is taken purely as a matter of course."

"You are here mainly for this purpose?"

"This, and as a contact for agents passing through to the Middle East or Europe. Now, on the day following the disaster I was asked by Peking for an interim report on the

67

naval situation here, and sent it, as usual, to Canton. I placed some emphasis, I recall, on the fact that one American destroyer of the Searcher class had left harbour a day before the disaster."

"This could mean nothing," I said. "They move almost daily between here and Taiwan."

"That is what I thought, but this particular destroyer never entered Taiwan. As you know, there is constant activity by the Seventh Fleet up and down the China coast, but on the disaster day there was nothing north of Taiwan except minor patrol elements. However, Taiwan agents reported that this destroyer — *Hunter*, I think she is called — did sail north as far as Quemoy, then unaccountably returned to Hong Kong, anchoring off Green Island."

"And you linked her with the explosion."

"Nobody is doing this. Any deviation from a given routine naturally interests observers. This deviation, coinciding with the terrible happening north of Canton as it did, caused specific inquiries to be made. I myself made the most searching inquiries into all naval movements and discovered nothing significant. And then, quite suddenly, an agent in Kowloon City reported that an American naval deserter was hiding there. This happens occasionally, of course. They run for various reasons, ranging from mere bar-girl escapade to religious intolerance of American policy in Vietnam." He grunted. "Perfectly understandable."

"A coloured man?"

"A San Francisco negro. The information came my way; I reported it as a matter of course. Decoding could hardly have taken place before I received another report from Kowloon City. The deserter was from a Searcher class destroyer; later it was established that he was one of the crew of the *Hunter*."

"You reported this also."

"Direct to Social Security in Peking. The effect was immediate. Advantage was taken of the mass emigration from Kwangtung to send in agents with the droves — you are one, and doubtless there are many others."

68

"Fifteen," I said, "all in charge of parties."

He moved uneasily. "But they will not all get here. The wastage is high."

"So I understand."

I went to the window. The tinsel rush of Wanchai flooded into me, though the refugee flood had largely diminished. Pole-bearers, their loads bouncing, bawled for a path; chattering school-girls with satchels and lollipops thronged the pavements in gesticulating, olive-skinned groups. Spewing from the cellars and attics of the shanties the flower-makers hurried under their gorgeous loads. On the sidewalks sat the morning beauty vendors, their paints and powders giving them the air of imperial queens, frantic fingers twisting in a tangle of bright ribbons and silver hair-trinkets. Smooth-bottomed harlots clip-clopped past, eyes cocked for sailors, Americans preferably. Hong Kong, shocked momentarily from its sea of pain into agony, had injected its serum of oblivion once again: life was subsiding to its normal standard of human misery.

I said, not turning from the window, "And they sent me to you for a reason?"

"Kwan To Lin sent you here to investigate the deserter."

"He might have mentioned this."

"Would you spread such business all over town? Supposing you had been caught?"

I said, "What about the other agents?"

"Many are already overdue – the British aren't fools, you know. Those who have arrived will be employed on this particular project. You have heard, for instance, of the Japanese Ku Ata and his Chinese partner Lum?"

I nodded.

"They were the first in, having the shortest route. Kwan To Lin came fifth, you were last – Hoon is the farthest point of emigration. Of the fifteen sent, nine have already been lost."

"It is a high casualty rate," I said, "and I am glad that Ku Ata and Lum got in safely. Are they in the city?"

"Kwan is safely in the city. Ku Ata and Lum are safely in Japan."

I stared at him, and he said, smiling, "This business may have many ramifications. Ku Ata is most important. Your investigation of the deserter is practically routine."

I scarcely heard him. I was thinking about Kwan. The knowledge that he was near brought me to a pitch of extravagant joy. I said:

"Where do I find this deserter?"

"He will find you."

"He will come here?"

Old Man said, "He will be here this evening, unaccompanied, and of his own accord. He has been given your name, told that you are a bar-girl, and advised that you will feed and shelter him until he can get a ship out of Hong Kong."

Old Man left me then, on some faint pretext that he had work to do in Kowloon. Strangely, I did not want to be alone. The very atmosphere of the room had a suffocating quality. This was my first assignment of importance. Were I to fail in this, I should be relegated to the back seats of the list. I knew agents, some quite successful ones, even men like Ku Ata and Kwan, who had been designated to positions of minor importance because of failure after a career of brilliance. It was so necessary to serve; this was the reason why one stayed alive. It was shatteringly lonely in the room, and I longed for Kwan in that loneliness: it was a savage hunger in the midst of perfumed idleness. I stared at the reflection: a bar-girl sitting in the glass.

Hating her, I turned the mirror aside and gazed out of the window.

Both Old Man and Lin Ho came and went during the day I spent waiting for the deserter. There was great discussion between them about Ku Ata and Lum, and of the organisation success that had got them into Japan. Old Man worked on papers, the woman brought in food and generally tidied around; neither appeared concerned with my existence, rather as if a bar-girl awaiting a coloured man in their room were part of an everyday occurrence. They spoke once of Kwan, but the talk was mainly of the Japanese Ku Ata, a man whose brilliance ran through the corridors of power, and it was stimulating to consider that I was sharing this project with such an agent. Nevertheless, it was perplexing to learn that Ku Ata was involved: his realm was nuclear physics, not common espionage. It was even stranger that he should be operating from Japan, and with the fanatical Lum. The combination was both intriguing and terrifying, and I wondered what Kwan thought of it. The day dragged on into afternoon and dusk. Old Man left at midday, but Lin Ho lingered until the neon signs began to flash. Plainly she did not like me. I spoke to her twice and she did not deign to answer. But she had timed events to a nicety. She had been gone but half-an-hour, and I was lying on the bed in abject boredom, when the negro came.

I was trapped in the falling void between sleeping and waking when he came in a thudding of footsteps up the stairs. The door rattled under his fist. Slowly I rose, opening it, and he stumbled past me just as I had expected, but he was hardly the man I had imagined. His great size seemed to fill the room, and the black coolie jacket and trousers he wore accentuated this; his eyes were round and white in the dim light of the window.

"Mei Kayling?"

"Yes, I am Mei Kayling."

He leaned against the door. "You take in men, ma'am?"

Crossing to the table I lit the lamp, closed the curtains and then turned up the wick. The room glowed with light. He said:

"Back in Kowloon City they said you took in men. They gave me this address." His voice quietened as he began to stare at me, his great, white eyes opening in bedsheet astonishment as they traced me from my head to my feet and back again.

71

"You got white hair," he said.

This did not perturb me; I was used to it. Strangely, too, it came as no great shock to see him standing there. In Peking University there was a coloured professor of English Literature, and I used to admire his cat-like grace, his slow, indolent manner of speech and scrupulous politeness.

"You Chinese, ma'am?"

"I am Chinese, but my blood is Eurasian."

He screwed at his hands. "You . . . you take me in? I won't be no bother to you."

"It will cost you money."

"Yes, I've got money."

"Where have you come from now?"

"I lived with a Chinese family, in Kowloon City."

I said evenly, "Are you running away from something?"

"They didn't ask that in Kowloon City."

I walked about, clutching my hands in feigned anxiety. "It's different there. The Hong Kong police don't go in there much. Here it is dangerous."

"More dangerous in Kowloon City," he said. "The police are starting a sweep up there, that's why the people I was with told me to come to you."

It was a little pathetic, this cheating. One day he would probably learn that if ever the police swept Kowloon City they would do so at the risk of war with China, for this was pure Chinese soil, and always had been.

"What is your name?" I asked.

"Dick Wain."

"American?"

"San Francisco."

"Off the ships?" I asked.

"Merchant Navy. I . . . I just want to lie up for a bit till I get a ship I'm waiting for. The *Euranus*. She's due in from Japan in eight days from now."

"You haven't killed anybody?"

"No." He stared at me with fugitive consternation. "Just that . . . well, I'm in a bit of trouble and I want to get clear."

72

"That will cost you more than ever. If I'm taking risks having you here, I shall have to be paid for it."

"How much?"

"Five hundred dollars."

"Hong Kong dollars?"

"Of course."

He took out a wallet and counted the notes on to the table. "In advance," he said. "For eight days, till the *Euranus* comes."

With the money paid he seemed to settle into the surroundings, wandering about looking at things. I watched him, unmoving.

"You work in the bars?" he asked.

"Does it make a difference?"

"Oh no, I didn't mean that. Just that ... well, you don't look like a bar-girl."

"Perhaps it is my hair?"

"Sure, sure, it's your hair."

I filled the kettle for coffee; he was watching my hands with meticulous care, smiling.

"You got beautiful hands," he said. "I've never seen any woman with such beautiful hands. Where do you work?"

"The Ho Tai." I looked at my watch. "I'm due there in an hour."

"Where's that?"

"In Jaffe Street."

"I've never been in that one," he remarked.

"It's a Chinese bar. Few Americans get in there." I poured coffee into cups. It was instant coffee and he probably wouldn't like it, but it was all Lin Ho had brought. Over my shoulder I said:

"Are you hungry?"

"Starved."

"You like Chinese food? It's all I've got."

"I'm that hungry I'd like anything." His accent was strange. It was the softest, roundest American I had ever heard.

73

I said, "I'll cook you something before I go to the Ho Tai. By the way, my mother comes in sometimes. Don't be afraid if she comes while I'm away."

"She lives here?" He was looking at the bed.

"She lives in Kowloon, she's a waitress in Sun Ya, and she comes here sometimes. She doesn't come in when the knocker is round the wrong way."

"When you've got men in?"

"That's right."

He sat down on the bed, watching me while I made the coffee. "Seems a pity that a girl like you has to live this way."

"There are stranger ways of earning a living in Hong Kong."

"But you're educated, you speak English fine."

"So do hundreds of other Chinese girls, but that doesn't keep them out of the bars."

This silenced him and he moved to the table, sitting there in frowning concentration while I laid it with bowls and chop-sticks. It was the knowledge of prostitution, of course; men are such appalling hypocrites. A glance, a smile, and he would have followed me to a bed like the rest of his kind, yet now he was enjoying his virtuous disappointment on learning that I was a prostitute. This is perverted self-betrayal; Kwan used to do it: the preservation of an ideal for their own personal desecration.

"I have a family to keep back in China," I said. It was the all-time excuse that worked the all-time magic. They forgave you anything as long as you had a family to keep back in China; somehow it laid all sins squarely at the door of the Communists and left everybody free to enjoy the night and money. We ate the simple meal of boiled rice and chopped fish with little comment, and as I washed up the bowls he wandered the room, hands thrust deep into his trouser pockets. The coolie clothes were sizes too small for him, and this brought upon him the impression of black nakedness, his muscles bulging and swelling with every movement, a stifling show of power. Behind the window the

74

street was waking for the night revelry in tyre-howl and traffic thunder. I said:

"I'm late, I must be going."

"When you coming back?"

"About three o'clock."

"What do we do for beds?"

"You have that one, I'll make up another when I come in."

"Got a toilet round here?"

"On the first landing, but be careful – many people use it."

He approached me. "And you won't give me away?"

"Of course not."

"Easiest thing in the world, you know. You might even hear talk about me when you get in the bar. And d'you know something? You haven't even asked what I'm hiding for."

"It is not my business," I said. "Besides, I have to live in Hong Kong after they take you away. That would not be easy."

"You reckon I'm safe here?"

"All the time you pay me money."

"That's straight enough."

I picked up my handbag and stood by the door watching him while he curled up on the bed like a gigantic cobra.

"Bring back some cigarettes?"

"Yes."

"Good night," he said.

Lin Ho was at the bottom of the stairs.

"He is upstairs," I said.

"Of course. That is why I am here."

"You'll watch until I come back?"

"I will see that somebody watches. If he attempts to leave he will be followed."

I said, "I am going to the Ho Tai because Old Man instructed, but I think it is ridiculous – while I am gone he could easily slip away."

She said, "It is essential to act normally. You are a bar-girl, and they stay in the bars until three o'clock. Besides, you will find Kwan To Lin waiting there."

75

Her words brought me to a state of trembling excitement and she peered at me in the street lights. "You know Kwan To Lin well?"

"He is a passing acquaintance."

"Keep it like that. Keep your mind on the job in hand. Kwan, they tell me, has a profound effect on women."

I bowed to her. "Until three o'clock," I said.

She was still watching me when I turned the corner of Queen's Road and Central.

CHAPTER EIGHT

The Ho Tai was on the corner of Jaffe Street within sight of the Praya. I walked slowly through the night crowds under the neon lights, pushing my way through a shoving, raucous mass of protest and hunger. Beggars called from the kerbs, children with bandaged eyes walked in circles of blind man's buff. Joss-sticks burned in papered windows. Laden with night-soil the Perfumed Ladies of the Night, one of Hong Kong's tourist attractions, shovelled and sweated at their bins. The sleek limousines of the rich thrust their chromium bonnets through the crowds in major and minor organ chords of threat, their occupants pale images on glass — wealthy merchants of the rape of Peking, expatriates from the little terraced houses of the west, now white-breasted in evening dress, their women fussing with excitement, viewing, through sliding windows, the putrifying lakes of Aberdeen and Shaukiwan. The bars and massage parlours were full, but the Ho Tai bar was empty. I opened the door to the blaze of the street and slammed myself into almost total darkness.

Constant appeals by the Reform Club of Hong Kong for better lighting in such establishments had been given the necessary publicity by the Government, and left at that. Though Hong Kong was the harlot of the east, it was imperative to make an official show; a few prosecutions here and there, but never enough to interfere with Hong Kong's revenue, which is largely obtained through drugs and vice. I groped through the tables, a darkness lit only by the glow of an occasional cigarette, towards the bar. A girl was sitting there on a high stool. As my eyes became accustomed to the darkness she grew into beautiful shape. Her legs, I remember, were long and white, and the gilt cheongsam she wore was split to the thigh. Her face was proud, her high forehead and flared nostrils telling of a northern tribe.

"Mei Kayling?" She said this in English, for there is a Chinese derivative.

I nodded, and she stubbed out a cigarette and climbed down from the stool.

"This way," she said.

To my surprise she led me back into the room, sitting me at a high-backed table in a corner. Her ridiculously long bangle earrings dangled before me as she leaned over the table.

"You want Mamasan?"

"I wait here for Mamasan," I said.

"You come for job?"

"I already got job," I said.

I was sickening of this. There was too much talking. The Americans might be naïve, but even they would not have conducted their espionage assignations in tinsel dives in alleys. The best way to avoid suspicion would have been to have met in the foyer of the Mandarin or Hilton, one of us a little drunk.

But I was intrigued by the Ho Tai bar.

I had never been in a bar before, but agents from Taiwan brought news of western influences there: of the night-lounging on neon-lit promenades; the fantastic standards bought with American money and Chinese virtue; the drink and prostitution that seemed to appear with everything American from Kobe to South Vietnam. A philosopher once said that if ever the world was in need of an enema, Hong Kong would be the point of insertion; one did not need

77

Taiwan as an example of western decadence through which the western world will die.

The girl was back on the high stool, and when Kwan entered he immediately went to her. I sighed. She spoke in rapid whispers. Kwan turned. Coming to my table he sat before me, smiling in the dusk with a sort of dreamy exultation.

"Good evening," he said.

It was a planned greeting of understatement, and I wanted to tell him to go to the devil. I thought it was a disgusting place to meet, among such women. But I was trembling, and not with indignation. The chemists relate that the human body contains in value about one yuan fifty of basic chemicals. This I can believe, and hated my weakness. No human being should be permitted to have such a devastating effect upon another.

"I could think of better places to meet," I said.

"The place is not important, it is the people who meet."

"You live here?"

"Of course not." He lit a cigarette. "Has he arrived?"

I said, "He came this evening. It was perfect timing."

"I assume he is being watched?"

"The woman Lin Ho is on watch, but it is not good that he stays alone for long."

"Has he told you anything yet?"

I said, "Of course he hasn't. I have had him exactly one hour. He appears an intelligent man, and it is going to take time."

Kwan was astonishingly handsome, the red light bringing his face to nobility and grace. I closed my eyes, turning away.

"Time is the essence, Kayling, you realise this?"

"If it's as important as that, he'd talk quicker if we got him over the border."

"There is no chance of that, the border has now been sealed."

"We could get him out by junk," I said.

78

"No. The sea is thick with British patrol boats. Hundreds of refugee junks are being turned back daily, we should never get him north. Nor must he be harmed, for this is as much diplomacy as espionage. The Politburo does not want an international incident over one man. When we hand him over to the American authorities he must go back intact."

"In eight days a ship comes in from Japan. He intends to be on it."

Kwan nodded. "Ah yes, the *Euranus*. This is what he told the people in Kowloon. She's bound for South America. He knows what he's doing, this negro. So do the naval authorities. They want him badly. You can't keep him in Wanchai for the next eight days – Old Man tells me they are starting a combined drag-net, taking in the whole of the city."

"When?"

"It begins tomorrow night, so you'll have to get him away."

"Where to?"

"Macau. And he will have to be moved tonight. This is why I sent for you. I have made all necessary arrangements. There is a junk out of Aberdeen at two o'clock tomorrow morning, and you will go with him. There are no complications, and it will be a very simple business. The junk-master is Chu-Lai. He has been briefed and he can be trusted. You know Coloane Island?"

"Every inch of it." I added, "My mother is buried there."

"Lin Ho is arranging transport, Old Man the details. A private taxi will be in Spring Garden Lane at one o'clock. The driver knows the position of Chu-Lai's junk."

"Supposing the negro will not agree to go?"

"It is inconceivable. He agreed readily enough to move from Kowloon – I am not concerning myself with this, Kayling, it is up to you."

"You mentioned British patrols," I said.

"The British are patrolling exodus waters from China, they cannot be everywhere at once."

He called for Chinese wine served hot, and this we sipped

in the half-darkness. This was the Kwan I admired, the leader of the Junior School of Espionage; his genius lay in his scrupulous attention to detail. He said:

"This man grows in importance with every passing minute. The measure of his importance is the frantic efforts the Americans are making to get him back. This is no ordinary deserter, even the Central Committee accept this now." He lowered his voice. "You should know the latest reports, Kayling. All Searcher class destroyers of the American fleet based on Taiwan are capable of nuclear delivery."

"I thought this was confined to Polaris?" Shocked, I stared at him.

"This has just come out. Your negro is causing an awful lot of backwash."

"Then it might have been an atomic attack?"

"It is not even being considered," he said acidly.

"But things begin to point that way."

"They do not − not on the basis of the information we have to date. The negro's background is being investigated. Reports are still coming in via the Central Office of Communication based on Canton. All American agents are insistent that he comes from a highly moral family and has had a good up-bringing, tending to the religious − most of them are the same."

"He lost a young brother in the San Francisco racial troubles, I hear."

"I don't know where Old Man got that from, but I certainly don't believe it."

"I will try to establish this."

"It could have a bearing on intention. What is his name again? I know him only as a number, and it is most impersonal."

"Dick Wain."

"It is a handsome name, I pray he is a handsome fellow. After all, if one has to extract personal secrets it is better to be happy doing it."

The flippancy was returning; it was typical of Kwan.

He looked at me, smiling. "And while on personal things, have you missed me?"

"Not particularly. On the road from Hoon it was hardly practicable."

"You did well, Kayling, The Committee is impressed. You lost only one, I hear – a child?"

"I lost nineteen," I replied. "You are wrongly informed. It was the blindness."

"But none through negligence. In return for this you brought in nearly two thousand. Even Ku Ata himself did not better this."

I could have wept with pride.

"And I have reported accordingly. I was wondering if we might celebrate this?"

It was inevitable. All Kwan's suggestions started basically moral, to degenerate as the night proceeded.

"Celebrate it?" I was not going to make it easy.

He lifted his glass. "I know a select little hotel on the road to Stanley. It is quite isolated and serves the most delicious chow-fan, also excellent European wine."

"Is this wise, at such a time?"

He gestured. "If carried out with the utmost propriety."

"And my deserter?"

"Men are most generous to one another, he would surely wait two hours."

"Answer to Peking, Kwan, if he has gone when I return."

"Answer to me, Kayling."

"Love has a place in most women's lives, Kwan, but at the moment I have more important things to do."

"And I am so free tonight. This is a tremendous waste." It was the way he looked at me.

It was an astonishing show of strength. Later, examining the situation, I was quite amazed. I remember that I saw him through the glaze of my lifted glass, for the lights had come on at the bar-counter behind him. And I saw, too, beside his smiling face the dark silhouette of the girl in gold, her head back in a flurry of laughter. There was consolation in knowing that he would have to have her checked, of course: her home, her family, her antecedents, to say nothing of her background. With half Social Security lying under the bed, intercourse, to Kwan, could never be taken lightly. Now he said, with measured charm:

"There are others readily available, you know." He inclined his head to the bar.

I rose, bowing. "Then I must share such pleasures, Kwan. Enjoy yourselves. Good night."

CHAPTER NINE

Lin Ho was waiting at the bottom of the stairs when I got back to the house in Spring Garden Lane.

"He is still upstairs?" I asked her.

"Of course."

I glanced around. "You already know about going to Macau?"

"Before you left here tonight. Kwan has his own way of working."

"Where is Old Man?"

"At Aberdeen, with Chu-Lai, the junk-master."

I looked at my watch. "He sails at two o'clock. This gives us two and a half hours."

"I will have the taxi in Queen's Road at one o'clock precisely. Be careful. Police patrols have been going through. The longer he waits outside the more dangerous it is."

I nodded, and ran up the stairs to the top floor. The door opened on its chain, slowly, quietly.

"It is Kayling!"

He locked the door behind me. "You're soon back. Didn't you go to the bar?"

He was rumpled with sleep and sweating badly, unusual for his race in this summer humidity, and I wondered in sudden panic if he was going to be ill.

I said: "I was in the bar only a few minutes. The place was full of American police. Why didn't you tell me you were a deserter?"

"Is it important?"

"It is to me. If the police find you here they will beat me almost to death."

I walked about, clutching at my hands, wondering if he believed this show of fear, for I was no actress. Even in the little Revolutionary plays of the university they always relegated me to minor roles where I could do least damage.

He said, "I suppose you forgot the cigarettes."

"I am very sorry."

He went to the window, standing with his back to me. "Well, what happens now? Do you turn me in?"

I said, "You have got to get away from here."

He turned instantly. "Where to?"

"Anywhere – Macau is the best place."

"Why?"

"Because early tomorrow they are bringing a drag-net through Wanchai."

"You heard this in the bar?"

I nodded. "I could get you into the New Territories, perhaps, but you would not have much chance. Everybody is being stopped with the immigrants flooding in."

"How far is Macau?"

"About thirty miles." I added, "My uncle is a junk-master and he makes the trip weekly. He's due out of Aberdeen early tomorrow morning."

He said, "What about the *Euranus*?"

"I asked about her. You were wrong about the date. She doesn't leave Kobe until ten days' time – Butterfield's say she's due in here on the fifteenth."

"That's a heck of a long time."

"That's what they said. I don't know the shipping movements. I only know that you can't stay here." I turned to face him. "Look, why don't you give yourself up?"

"Oh no, they're not getting me."

83

"Then you'll have to go to Macau. Shall I come too?"

He smiled slowly. "I can see this is going to cost me money. Can you get away from the bar?"

"Of course."

"Don't the Chinese do anything free?"

"Not when they're as poor as I am."

"How much?"

"Another five hundred dollars. My uncle will take us to Macau and fetch us back in time for the *Euranus*."

"What about passports, and all that?"

"You won't need a passport on Coloane."

"Where's that?"

"An island just south of Macau, near the Chinese mainland."

"Wouldn't that be dangerous, considering I'm black?"

"That's why you'd be safer there than here. Black Mozambiques garrison Macau and the islands, though they're mostly on Taipa."

"We'd never get through the screen," he said. "It'll be thick with patrols between here and Macau."

"You pay the money," I replied, "and leave that to my uncle."

He paid the dollars on to the table, pausing with a smile as he saw me watching the money. He said softly:

"And when this runs out, I suppose you'll turn me in?"

"More than likely."

"Dog eat dog."

"Now you are finding out what it is like to be Chinese," I said. "This wasn't our game in the beginning; it was people like you who taught us how to play it."

Sweat was on my face. I raised a hand and wiped it away. It was damnable, this anxiety sweating.

"It could be cheap at the price," he said softly, "you and me on the island of Coloane."

"That part of it won't cost you a cent," I replied, going to the door.

"Where you goin'?"

84

"To arrange things with my uncle."

He sat down on the bed, nodding sagely. "Running to the first Snowdrop you can find?"

I said, "If you look at the table you'll see I haven't even picked up the money."

I shut the door and ran down into the street. Lin Ho was on the other side of the road, looking in a window. She turned, but made no sign that she had seen me.

I walked slowly through Wanchai and along the wall of Victoria barracks as far as the Hilton. It was necessary to waste time lest the negro's suspicions were aroused. Before the China Bank the square was packed with people, and at Star Ferry the refugees poured in, many of them blind, most of them burned. The pavements were thronged with casualties and Red Cross doctors and nurses knelt among them, bathing, bandaging under the street lamps. Food kitchens had been set up by the Salvation Army and Street Sleepers' Association. Ambulances arrived, were filled to overflowing, and speeded away to Happy Valley where a temporary medical centre had been organised by the Military. People jabbered as they passed me, their voices shrill with horror, sirens wailed. I wondered what was happening in Peking. Its statesmen were unusually quiet in the grip of this phenomenon, but I knew the statesmen of Peking. Lin Piao of the Red Guard I knew personally; to Chou En-Lai I had often spoken; even to the great Mao Tse-tung I had bowed in private: I knew these fearless men. If America was at the root of this calamity in Kwangtung, then America would know a modern war on her doorstep. For every Chinese death ten Americans would die; for every nuclear explosion on Chinese soil ten nuclear explosions would ravage America, the enemy of the common man. In the last analysis of power the soldier with the rifle would triumph; this Chairman Mao had told us. The leaders in Peking would unravel the mystery and discover the truth. If the west was guilty then the west would perish.

After an hour I walked back into Wanchai.

At one o'clock that morning I led the negro down the stairs and into the waiting taxi: unseen, Lin Ho was working with her usual clockwork precision.

"Aberdeen," I said, and we slid through Wanchai on the road to Causeway Bay, then turned right under a raging moon for the gap of Aberdeen. Here the fish labourers were playing fan-tan along the old stone quay; in grisly bundles of rags the labourers of the building sites squatted in dejection; the bony unloaders of San Tong and Shaukiwan whom Hong Kong had long since relegated to her human dustbin had lifted the lid and crept out to die. Now they sat in circles around their heroin lamps, sucking with coca-cola straws at the drug that diluted the terror of their lives. Swiftly I led the negro through them into a swaying forest of masts and spars.

"Chu-Lai?" The whisper went round the creaking hawsers and wave-lap.

"Third junk down the middle flow – Chu-Lai?"

"Ah!"

The moon *blazed*; the whole garish waterfront was coming to life with the advent of the negro; the Chinese do not miss much. Hoklo wives chattered amid the desecration of their pots and pans, nudging, pointing; naked children crawled from sampan hatches to sit and stare; verminous grand-fathers, too old to die, peered from carved Tan-gar faces, and family groups in chop-stick relish and belches raised gusty tirades; can-fires were poked in discontent, red sparks sailed against the stars. It was the old story: who had caused the Kwangtung disaster, how many blind had entered Hong Kong since the Big Light.

"God, what a place!" said the negro.

I paused on a sagging plank, reached backwards and hauled him on through the stinking acreage of rotting hulls, through the staring faces. Beyond this festering place kept by the Government as a tourist attraction the fish restaurant of Tai Pak glowed red and gold in the ebony waters, and the furtive, harlot moon beamed silver over the bay where the junks and sampans battered and heaved to the rolling tide.

"Hurry!" I whispered.

On the fringe of the moorings we climbed a last gang-plank and hand-sprang over the gunwale of Chu-Lai's sea-junk. A sail instantly unfurled above us; the diesel started in a cloud of smoke, and thumped under our feet. Commands were whispered, coolies flung ropes in berserk labour, and the prow swung over the blaze of Tai Pak. The big junk heeled, scenting a tack, then settled into the belly of the sea and turned her nose west, to Macau.

The negro did not speak. His great, white eyes were staring at me in the vivid light of the moon.

A wasteful wind moaned eerily across the yellow waves of Macau, the flat-fisher junks savaged the mountain rim of distant China: even in this faint light, for the moon was spent at the thought of dawn, I could see the jagged promenade of the *Praia Grande*, and the dim lights winked and beamed from the temple gardens of Barra and Mong-Ha. Coloane came up through the night then, its threatening mass fringed with yellow sand and phosphorescent surf, most beautiful. In her east channel a red light searched. The negro pointed.

"Gunboat patrol," he said.

I shouted for Chu-Lai and he came merrily, his sun-hat still on the back of his head.

"Chinese patrol," he said. "She will not worry us. Tell him we are one of hundreds."

We slid down the gap between the islands then, the flat-fishers creeping past us in ghostly mist and tattered sails, and took west again to the south of Coloane. Chu-Lai anchored her off a sandy inlet a hundred yards from shore; the coolies hung out the save-life sampan and packed in food-boxes. All this the negro saw, and did not speak. Now he sat in the prow of the sampan while I ferried it for the shore with the oar-sweep, and the moon flashed quicksilver along the breakers of the beach. Surf-roar and tide-swell, the shingle screamed. I drove the sampan hard up on the sand and the negro leaped out and pulled her high, and we saw, waiting to greet us, a bleached mare's skull on the sand, its eye-sockets filled with light, glowing like the eyes of a dog. The negro stared, his hands to his face, but I caught his arm and dragged him after me up the beach while he lagged like a child, staring at the mare's skull.

"They're ten a dollar, this is Coloane!" I cried above the surf.

Together we laboured, dragging out the food-boxes, the fishing-lines and lobster-cages.

"You have been here before?" he asked.

"When I was young. We lived here."

"How far is China?" He straightened, turning to stare, looking magnificent against the emblazoned sea, for the moon had got her skirts above her knees again and the world was brilliant.

"About three miles."

"That's too close for comfort."

"Safer than in Wanchai."

"Where are we staying?"

I laughed at him. "In a mat-shed."

"What's that?"

"You'll soon see." I took a last haul on the sampan line. "Come."

It was necessary for me to pay immediate tribute to my mother, for tomorrow was the anniversary of Ching Ming, which is the festival of sweeping the graves, but I could not go. How could I go up the hill to the grave of my mother with a man of strange colour, and at night? Together we walked along the beach, our feet splashing in the tide-swim, and the derelict mat-shed where once I fished sagged above us in a tangle of spars and tattered ropes. We touched the spindly cranks and masts, all barnacled and cobbled with sea-shells and weed.

"You know this old shed?" he asked.

"Once I lived in this," I said. "When I was two years old

my mother brought me here from Hong Kong, and for a time we lived in such a mat-shed, fishing by day on the winch and working in the fire-cracker factories on the mainland."

"We living here now?"

"There's no hotel for you on Coloane."

We climbed the dunes to the entrance of the mat-shed. The door was off its hinges, broken timbers, rotting rope and skeins of cob-webbed fishing-net straggled a smashed buoy in a corner. The rush weave sagged, windowed by a thousand rents that pictured the stars, but it was shelter. There was a smell of dried fish and worm-casts in rusted cans, and I knew that not long ago this had been in use. I said, "You go and bring the food-boxes and fishing gear, and I will tidy it up."

"Gonna get wet if it rains." He prodded the ceiling.

"If it lets in too much rain we'll find a better one down the coast."

But he did not go for the gear immediately, and I leaned against the door-post watching him poke around the little room. He had taken off his coat and shirt, and the great breadth of his ebony shoulders seemed to dominate everything. He was child-like in this new environment, a simple, uncomplicated grace in his every movement, and there was in him a complete acceptance of this primitive, humble place. Turning with a wide smile, he said suddenly:

"Are there any hotels on the Macau mainland?"

"The Caravella, the Bella Vista — a score of others — take your pick. But you'll also have to take your chance."

"This is for me, they can keep their hotels. I like this place."

Kneeling, he pointed down the beach and I saw the mare's skull in the tide-swim, its phosphorous eyes flashing in sea-spray.

"You get rid of that?" he asked.

"If you like, but there'll be another one here tomorrow. Down this coast dozens are washed up. The old traders through the Barrier Gate brought in their barter on horses, and when they became too old for labour the Ports would load them on to junks, take them out to sea and tip them over, to save the cost of burying them. A hundred years later the skulls still come back to Macau."

He sat with his back against my legs, staring at the sea.

"It's good in this place," he said. "I like it better'n any place I've been."

"For a few days, until my uncle comes to fetch us back for the *Euranus*."

"You told him when to come back?"

"He knows the shipping better than me. He will come in time, don't worry."

"You realise you're still wearing that silver cheongsam?"

"I'll go and change it."

"No, don't. Don't do that." He got up, standing before me, and said, "If I get out of this alive I'll always remember you standing there in that cheongsam."

"What makes you think you will not get out if it alive?"

He shrugged, making a boyish face.

I said, "They don't kill you for being a deserter. When you get your trouble sorted out you can give yourself up."

He smiled with lazy tolerance and pushed me gently before him. "Let's do one thing at a time. All I want right now is sleep."

Kneeling, he flung himself outstretched, his head on his hands, staring down at the sea. I went to the sampan, returning with blankets. With one of these I covered him, for the wind was suddenly cold, then rolled up in the other. I expected him to turn then, reaching for me, but he did not. Instead, he slept in rhythmic breathing. I began to think about Kwan, and Old Man, and wondered whether he was now on the Macau mainland, for it was essential that I should maintain some source of contact. If Old Man was in Macau things would be easy. One could always go through the Barrier Gate and take a fast car to Canton, but this was dangerous, even for me. Little Caesars existed in the lower formations of Government; there would be the eternal questions, the refusal to accept official passwords and codes, all of which had been agreed at such border posts. A leak of security would be unforgivable at such a time. I watched the negro. He slept with animal grace, a primitive stain on the rush floor of the hut. The sea crashed and screamed on the shingle, the night went on in patterned moonlight crossing the room. Later the wind rose to a higher note, buffeting in cold flushes across the steepled dunes; thunder rose like an ogre in the mountains of the night and boomed and reverberated in the peaks of beloved China. The mat-shed sagged beneath a torrent of rain, but still the negro slept. Presently I slipped into a void of shivering drowse, and when I awoke with the first light of morning I flung aside the blanket and stumbled to the door of the mat-shed, staring down at the beach, for the negro had gone.

CHAPTER TEN

When I reached the beach I saw the negro bathing in the sea: far out beyond the breakers he was swimming, gathering great tunnels of green water in his arms and driving them beneath him so that only his ebony shoulders and crinkled head made white foam, so quickly did he go. Distantly beyond him, although he could not see it, a Chinese patrol-boat was making speed, wallowing in the troughs with white down her wake, and in the eye of my mind I saw the binoculars slowly rise, fix the negro in the sea, and lower. As if commanded, the boat swung her prow east and made towards the slicing flounder-fishers whose bat-winged sails razored the white shore of the *Praia Grande*. I smiled. One might dislike the indolent attitude of Kwan To Lin, I reflected; one might censure his morals and examine his design for the good of the Republic; but nobody who worked with him could ever doubt his efficiency. I knew then that he had ordered Old Man to support me in Macau.

When the patrol-boat had gone I walked down to the sea. The negro saw me coming and waved, wading into the shallows with swinging shoulders and sluggish pulls of his thighs, as naked as ivory. Magnificent he looked, his great body gleaming and flashing in the dawn sunlight, and he stooped suddenly in childlike joy, gathering handfuls of sea and flinging it high, turning up his face to the pattering foam; a purer man than Yuen Sun Johnny. No woman could compare her body with this for symmetry and magnificence. He came on, laughing, and the sunlight rippled and flashed upon him, bringing him to a feline grace that I had never before seen on a human. Nor did he pause to consider this nakedness but ran up the beach to me, throwing himself gasping at my feet, thinking I knew of all men.

"Where you been?" he demanded.

I replied, "I was tired, and awoke late. I was frightened because I thought you had left me."

He just sat there, peering up into the sun. The tide swam between us.

"You see the patrol-boat?"

"I saw a boat far out at sea."

He nodded. "Chinese patrol. I saw enough of those off Taiwan with the Seventh. Chinese, all right, though I don't know why she didn't come in — she must have seen me."

I replied, "They see all things. Sometimes they interfere, sometimes they do not. Usually they are nosey pigs."

"Why didn't she come, then?"

I pulled my cheongsam above my knees and squatted down beside him. "Perhaps they thought you were one of the big Mozambiques come over from the fort, down here with his girl from the *Beca da Roza*, a pataca woman."

"A pataca woman?"

The sea poured hot trickles on my toes. There was a sensuous warmth in squatting here beside the negro, his shining body moulded in bright sand. I replied, "This would be a chuck-a-luck girl or one living in the houses of prostitution, and for her the big black Mozambiques would pay about two or three patacas a night over here on Coloane — about fifty cents or so your money."

"They would come here?" He rose on an elbow.

I nodded. "They'd be like us — living in one of the old fishing-gambles on here or Taipa. There is no difference between me and them, really. They are pataca women, I am a dollar woman. And they would live together as we are doing, lazing all day, fishing along the beaches, and every time he took her for his pleasure he would pay her one pataca for the priest, one for her mother and father and another for her grandmother back in China — they all have grandmothers back in China."

"Are they all Chinese?"

"No. Some are Macanese. It is better for these girls because if they fall on bad times they can get *assistência* from the Macau Government. But there is no help for the Chinese girls, so it is work for the firecrackers or under the tourists down the *Beca da Roza.*"

"Do the Chinese girls smuggle in?"

"Mostly," I replied. "Some because they have relatives here, some because they hate the Communists, and others because they need the heroin and they can get it easier and cheaper in Macau since it is banned in Red China. First they go into the bars and sing. Later they go into the balcony houses and drink Casel Garcia and Mateus Rosé, and if they aren't on the game when the bottles are full they are when the bottles are empty."

"Reckon you know Macau," he said.

"I told you, I lived here. Between the ages of two and ten. When I was six I used to go with the other children down the lane of Roses and watch the prostitutes at work with the tourists. There were many holes in the wall covered with sheets, and an old woman calling the prices: six patacas an hour for the girl in number one, five patacas for the girl in number two — as you went down the street the price got less. And sometimes the wind would blow and a bedsheet curl up and all the children would shriek and point and the old man would come swearing and cursing and driving us away. When we had finished with the fun there we would go to the next street and watch the heroin mainliners and others buying the Ruby Queen cigarettes and Poor Man's powder, and then on to the *Rua da Felicidade* and watch the church processions coming around the *Praia Grande* up to St. Paul's cathedral. I can smell the incense now and see the priest in his silk and finery; it was very beautiful."

"Tell me more about it," he said.

I got up, walking about. "There is not much to tell. Sometimes we lived in a fish-gamble like this. When I was five years old my mother put me into the firecracker factory up at the Barrier Gate. There were eight other children there and the table was round, I remember. The firecrackers would be in a big dish in the middle of the table, in bundles, and each child would take a bundle, untie them and spread them out for closing."

He peered, head on one side. I said, "We had a steel closing tool. A man would fill each cracker and the children would close the ends of them. Children are best for this work because they have nimble fingers. I used to close about a thousand a day and take home about two patacas, with blisters on my fingers through the gunpowder burns. My sister Chieh used to work with me; she was two years older."

"Your sister Chieh?"

"She was true Chinese. Every night my mother used to burn paper money down on the beach to help ancestors who were in debt in the Afterworld. The money used to cost twenty cents a bundle, and I used to watch it go up in smoke. We worked ten hours a day, Chieh and I."

"You must have had a terrible childhood."

"Some had worse. We never got an explosion. One time in Macau there were so many maimed children on the streets that the tourists complained, and some of the firecracker factories moved to Taipa. Nor did we catch the gunpowder cough. If you work with the powder too long you get it on the chest and die with tuberculosis." I said, "But this is stupid, I am telling you everything about myself and I don't know anything at all about you."

94

"You do," he said. "I'm starving. Is there anything for breakfast?"

Reaching up, he gripped my hands and pulled himself to his feet. No fool, this one. Kwan used to say that in the last resort an oyster is opened with a knife, but many, more intelligent than others, might be persuaded to open of their own volition. I liked this negro. It seemed terrible to have to take him to the mainland. Now, hand in hand – and this was his idea – we walked down the beach and climbed the dunes to the fish-gamble.

We had tins of food, but, boyishly, he wanted to try the net first, so we wound up on the winch and there was one fish tangled in the skein, a big fat flounder all silver and terror. The negro, now in shirt and trousers, watched with great white eyes as I killed, gutted and skewered it over a flame. He said:

"You think they'll be through Wanchai by now?"

"Who?" I turned the fish with tremendous concentration.

"The police?"

"The police? Oh yes, certainly."

He watched me studiously while I knelt and blew the embers into a blaze and the flounder frizzled and spat at us and we protested, hands shielding our eyes, and laughed together, prodding him with chop-sticks. The dawn sun climbed red and glorious and singed molten in a sea of cobalt blue. The day flamed into life. Mist grew on the horizon, sweat dripped down the face of Macau. The negro said:

"Maybe I shouldn't have left that ship, but there was nothing else to do."

I wiped the plate with black bread, running my finger round the rim for the fat, and sucked it noisily. "Don't you like it here, then?"

He did not hear this, being lost in thought.

"Eh?"

I said, "Perhaps you do not like it here with me."

"It's better here than any place I've been."

"Then why do you talk of dirty old Hong Kong?" I held up the backbone of the flounder. "You see this? He was Macanese. In the New York restaurants they would pay perhaps one U.S. dollar for him, golden and brown."

Rising with indolent grace he went to the window and gripped the sill, staring out. I said:

"You will be all right when I go to Coloane market for fresh vegetables this afternoon?"

"Of course."

I clattered the eating-bowls, saying, "If you will give me some money I will buy rice noodles and pork meat, and from these I can make pies on a two-pataca cooking stove. Tomorrow we will catch crabs and shrimpies. It is good to have fresh fish, but first I must check with the villagers before we eat more, lest it is poisoned."

This turned him. "Poisoned?"

"Because of the Big Light that came on the mainland."

"What is that to do with it?"

"The water may be radio-active."

"How can that be? There was no fall-out." He turned away.

"You know this?"

"Of course I know it. The papers said so."

"They did not say this in the Hong Kong papers — not in Chinese. You get a big bomb and you get things poisoned, this is what they say."

"Then they're wrong. It was clean, and limited. There was a graphite slow-down on the neutrons. No reaction, no contamination, it was clean."

"Then we can eat the fish without worry?"

"Sure you can eat the fish."

I said, "Today you are like a big grumpy bear and I do not like you. I say only what the papers say, and I do not know what I am talking about. You know about these things. You should not be angry with me."

He left me and walked down on to the beach, squatting in broody isolation, so I stayed and washed the bowls in the tide, leaving him to his disconsolation. Later I joined him, and he said:

"When the *Euranus* comes in your uncle Chu-Lai will fetch me at once?"

"At once."

"That's good. I like it here with you, but a man must plan. I will stay in South America for a few months only, then try to get up north, back to San Francisco. It is better to be with one's own people."

"Of course." I lay on my elbow beside him in the sand.

"But it was right to leave that destroyer. How can one live one's life without a single protest?"

"My life has been one long protest," I replied. "You make protest because you are coloured?"

"That might have something to do with it."

I said, "That is a protest based on self-pity, and I have no time for it."

"Woman, you might think different if you were me."

I sat up. "You are lucky, really. At least you are pure in nationality, and I think your colour is beautiful, but you know what the Chinese say? God put men in the oven of life and cooked them for the world, and some he over-did black, which was a mistake: some he under-did, and they came out white, which was another mistake. Only the Chinese he did correctly, in the oven of the sun, and we came out golden."

He grinned again, showing his white teeth. "But you're more the colour of an Indian woman."

"That is because I am two nationalities – see my hand on your arm, it is the hand of a brown ghost. My mother was Tan-gar, which is aborigine blood, my father was fair English. I am not Chinese, so the Chinese hold their noses as I pass, for Europeans stink to Chinese noses. I am not British, so the British turn up their noses as I pass: they despise the Chinese because of their peasant habits, their religions and their worship of the dead – anything the European doesn't understand he despises. But it is astonishing how despicable a human being can be and yet be

97

treasured. Between sheets I have no smell, no peasant habits, no heathen religion, and no nationality. It is quite astonishing, this treasuring, this marvellous equality. It is one of the compensations of prostitution."

"I've been a pig to you, I'm sorry," he said.

"It is all right," I replied, "do not be sorry."

"It is just that I pity you."

"It is you who should be pitied. With all your advantages you are on the verge of tears while I am on the tip of laughter. Is it so bad, being coloured?"

Gripping my wrist, he pulled me flat on the sand beside him and leaned above me, his arm encircling my waist with sudden, terrifying strength. It was like being in the grip of a gigantic ape, and it silenced me. He said:

"You are strange and wonderful, Mei Kayling. At first I suspected you, now I do not."

"But why should you suspect me?"

"Because I came from the destroyer."

I laughed at this. "I have had many men, and always they come from the American warships, so what is this?"

"It is not important," he said. "Soon I will make love to you."

"Now you are being sensible. This is very important. When?"

"Now?"

"Not now," I said, and fought myself free of him in a flurry of laughter. With one hand he could have held me, but did not. "Later," I cried, twisting away, "after I have gone to Coloane."

He kissed me, and the kiss stilled the nonsense in me. In the moon-glow of his big, round eyes he kissed me.

"Tonight, then, when you come back from Coloane."

Nor might it be tonight, though I did not tell him this. Today was the festival of Ching Ming, which is a sweeping of the graves. Tonight, before the rise of the moon, I might be visiting my mother.

98

Before noon I left the fish-gamble with the negro standing in the doorway, and took the road to Coloane, hating myself. It was a tremendous game of the English Judas.

The mountain was alive and fanning bright green in the sea-wind, and the great outcrops of the China islands flashed strickening light from an incinerating sun. From a high point on the mountain trail I looked down at the golden lip of the beach where the trees waved, and saw the negro still at the door of the gamble, and I feared for him. I feared that the big fish-flounders of Macau might see him and come cutting in with billowing sails, for here, they would think, was a black Mozambique down from the Portuguese fort with his *Salazar* girl, and in his pockets would be money for the gaming tables of the casinos. Maybe, when I returned, he might be gone. For this crime Kwan would surely have to kill me. This thought fevered me, and I hurried along the trail and down the hill to the Coloane jetty, and the shore of Macau grew from the sea, a sardonic grin of palatial houses.

The ferry was in when I reached the jetty where the aged buffaloes of Coloane, awaiting loading for the slaughter-houses of the mainland, moved in restless agitation in a reek of splash droppings and urine, their bowels turning to water, for blood was on the wind. Here, when I was a child, amid the thuds and commands of the ferry loadings, the twins Jennie Hak Tin and Li used to beg, aged seven, their eye-sockets red in the sun, the refuse of the cracker factories of Barra. And Pattie Rea, aged twelve, a child vixen with a tongue like a cobra, used to solicit the Chinese labourers, she being fair in the skin and with bright hair, like mine, and therefore much desired. And the Andres family? Where was the Andres family these days, I wondered? Where were they now, these ghosts?

But no ghosts were on the jetty now; only the tourists flocking ashore from the ferry, in white suits and bright dresses, the tall Americans with cameras swinging, transistor radios and nasal cries; soothing their petulant children, calming their dominant wives. In droves they came, like the cattle of the *Salazar*, pointing, snapping, shrieking their astonishment at the ordinary in a larger-than-life, artificial American dream. A few of the women stared at me, an impossible impertinence. Hawking deep in my throat I spat at their feet. Old Man, as I expected, was there. Sitting on a bollard he was staring at the ferry.

"Ah!" he said in his beard.

His very presence I found intolerable. The only pure thing on Coloane that day was a San Francisco negro. And the presence of the Americans was bringing me to a blinding, suffocating hatred I could hardly contain. Soon these, I reflected, with the bloated faces and socketed eyes of Kwangtung, would stare at things Chinese, and not see. The only argument such as these understood came out of the wrong end of a gun. Old Man said:

"An admirable detestation, Kayling. You are doing marvellously."

"I hate them!"

"Of course. It promises well. Our little black man on the beach must have told you something."

I replied, "I read between the lines."

"But he has not spoken?"

"He has not. Do I stand at the roots of his tongue? I have had him a few days."

"You will have to work faster, my dear. The Politburo will not like it."

"The Politburo will have to wait, and so will you."

"Understandable. It could be passably gay, lying all day on a golden beach in the arms of such a man. No doubt you will eventually stir yourself into a semblance of espionage."

"I shall not talk here among this scum. It is stupid, and dangerous."

"Of course. Meanwhile try to contain yourself. Look, they are going." He sighed deep. "On the bones of my ancestors, I say this. Kwan To Lin might have taught you how to untie knots, but if ever my old head rolls by order of the Central Committee it will be over the lap of another appalling actress."

I closed my eyes to a physical revulsion. This grew less, I found, as the Americans moved away.

"We will talk here," said Old Man. "It is ideal, in full view of the crowd, the stupid, lumbering crowd. Sit at my feet, and be a dutiful daughter."

I sat at his feet and grew into the challenge and noise about me, the beat of the sun, the shrieks of the labourers, the white duck frothing of the ferry. Little schoolgirls in green jackets and black ties snaked up the hill in the viper strike of my vicious dream. I looked to the east. The last of the white-clad Americans were straggling over the hill to the village. I took a deep breath of relief and turned my face to the sun.

"There," said Old Man, "that is surely better." He filled his silver-bowled pipe with careful fingers. "If this man does not talk pertinently tomorrow I shall have to take him to the mainland, you know."

"That would be short-sighted."

"Political madness. The Americans must have him back intact." He glanced down at me, stroking my hair. "A point I would ask you to consider, with night coming on, and a full moon."

"Where is counter-intelligence?"

"On Macau, without a doubt. They tell me everybody is going quite mad in Hong Kong, trying to find him. The wires are alive between here and America, the air is jammed with morse. From Manhattan to Cuba every agent in Social Security is looking under the table. Kobe is being combed, Osaka ransacked, according to reports. A very, very important negro." He turned my face to his. "And Kwan came through this morning. Your young man, it appears, was projectile artificer on that destroyer."

"What is that?"

"His main task would be the arming of the rocket warhead. A very important procedure, but not the most important. With these devices locked and counter-locked it would have to be a very clever man to get an armed head through the screen of technical check — say during a drill action."

"I do not know what you mean," I said.

"Just this. If this atomic explosion was caused by the destroyer, the launching was either intentional or unintentional. To establish this is of the gravest importance. Assuming that the launching of an armed war-head was unintentional, then it would need somebody aboard that destroyer acting independently of the military requirement."

"You are saying that when an explosion occurred nobody was more shocked than the captain of the ship?"

"I am saying that when it happened the only man aboard the ship who was not shocked was your negro."

"You mean he planned it?"

"I do not mean that. In fact, I have no opinion in the matter because I am not a technician. I am quoting a scientific opinion. Peking is now assured that the missile came from this destroyer, and since we are now fully capable of nuclear retaliation it cannot be believed that America would be foolish enough to trifle with us. Our present handicap — and this will not last for long — is the problems involved in delivery of a nuclear strike. Now, perhaps, might be the best time for the west to act against us, but not in this limited manner — by total obliteration."

I said, "But coming back to the negro. Was he in a position to be able to arm such a device?"

"Most certainly, but he would need help. It would never be entrusted to a single man. The Americans may be immature, but they are not that foolish."

"So somebody else must be involved."

"Exactly."

"Aboard the ship, and on shore."

"Aboard the destroyer, my dear Kayling, ashore, in the atomic armament factory, the munition stores and possibly the Pentagon. We are back, I fear, to the hawks and doves, the big business enclave that runs American politics."

I said, "You are inferring now that it was intentional."

Old Man rose. "Whether it was intentional or not, they will get it back. If it was a stupid error of ship procedure and administration, it is still unforgivable. The nation that sails the coasts of another with atomic rockets cocked at the heart cannot afford such blundering, and America will pay the price. If it was planned and executed officially or by treason the effect is exactly the same – thousands killed, thousands blinded. At this moment in time your negro is the most important man in the world, Kayling. Lose him and you lose your life. Where is he now?"

"On the south beach."

"Keep him there. Find the missing link in the chain – there is somebody missing; there is somebody close to this negro who has actuated this explosion and left him to take the blame."

"And this is why he deserted?"

Old Man rose and stood before me, smiling. "This, to you, is a pleasing thought because you are a woman. Do not discount the possibility that this coloured man was a perfectly willing tool. Remember something – he may be coloured, but he is still an American."

A little wind moved from the sea, touching my face with perfumed fingers: the sun was boiling his lobster tourist faces. Sweat in bright fingers ran over the brown backs of the labouring coolies, and the buffaloes bellowed at the sky for water.

I asked, "How long have I got?"

Old Man said, "If today you learned the chain of responsibility, the names, the addresses and the political intention, and pinned it firmly on to the Pentagon with proof, you would still be late in the opinion of the Central Committee."

I stared at him. The spit came dry in my mouth. Old Man smiled.

"Yes, the Central Committee. Mei Kayling is suddenly an important agent. All heads roll on the whim of Mei Kayling. *Listen*. If you have no answers within three days I will take your negro to the mainland. There he will talk in seconds.

103

But it is not politically expedient that I do this. The original order stands. He goes back to the American authorities unharmed: this is good espionage."

I said, "Within three days I will come here again."

"Not here. By the steps of the Goddess Ama, the Temple."

I nodded, and we stared at the sky where white clouds were lumbering in panic before the molten onslaught of the noon sun, flying in quicksilver light for the caverns of grey that still hung in a faint mushroom over blinded Kwangtung. Old Man licked his dry lips.

"It is a beautiful day," he said, "a most beautiful day."

CHAPTER ELEVEN

In the market I bought a two-pataca oil stove for cooking, some rice, noodles and pork meat. On the way out of the market there stood before me with a ringed neck a little cormorant, bedraggled with surf oil, and skinny to have his bones out, and him I bought also for one pataca thirty-four os and his one foot in the grave. With the cormorant under one arm and my purchases under the other I turned my back on the Pearl River all flashing in the sun like crumpled silver paper. An ox lowed bassly from a mountain farm, and on the wind came the scent of udders and milk, which is a sweet, soft smell velvet to the fingertips, like the inside of a thigh. The sky was oystered and rippled with crimson as I climbed to the grave of my mother, which was fine for *Feng Shui* with its wind and water, and there I laid down my bundles and with the cormorant held against me knelt at the grave, and prayed. Soon, I promised her, when this task was over and China was served, I would return to this place, this being the eighth year of her tenancy, and draw her forth. With a Taoist priest of Macau I would come, which would pay tribute to my mother, and a labourer. I would expose the coffin and lift the lid. One by one I would take out her bones, first hiding the skull under my coat away from eyes. Then I would polish

104

the bones with sand, the little bones of the feet I would polish first and place them at the bottom of the Canton urn. Next the leg bones I would take, and these I would perfume, and lay them next in the urn: then the rib cage, the arms, the tiny bones of the fingers – all these I would place most carefully in the urn lest I bring her lop-sided in her Paradise. On these, amid the incantations of the priest, I would lay the skull and cover the mouth of the urn away from flies. All this I would do for my mother, though not really believing, for I am Red Guard. Perhaps, I reflected, my mother might have left a message for me in the coffin: this brought me to a wonderful excitement. Surely, the pieces of jade I would take and hole and thread in a necklace to wear next to my skin; these pieces which, at my mother's death, I had placed in the nine orifices of her body. And this jade necklace, which for eight years had prevented the entry of the evil ones into my mother, would then protect me. Later, I swept the grave with my hands, gathered little wild flowers from the scrub, and placed them around: then I prayed to my mother's gods, not to mine, for I have no gods now. I also wept, which was shameful. The sun was flaring in his sea of fire; crickets chirped and cicadas sang their hymn to summer as I went back to the south beach to seduce the negro.

He was awaiting me at the fish-gamble, this one, and by the side of the hut he had placed the white mare's skull on a driftwood pole.

"Thought you'd gone for good," he said.

"There were many people in the market." I threw the cormorant at his feet. "This one I brought as a friend, for it is better for two to be three."

At this he knelt, his hands out, his mouth making sweeting noises at the cormorant, which was terrified – I also, for our men do not make such noises.

"How much you pay for him?"

"About one pataca fifty. He will catch fish for us. See, he is skinny." I rolled the bird on to his back and pinched his chest. "It is one fish in seven for a fishing-bird, or he dies; they have been mean with him." I untied my bundle. "Here is a cook-stove, also noodles and rice and fresh pork meat for a fry. Tonight we will eat like pigs and bust."

"You are changing," said the negro.

I glanced up. "Why do you say that?"

He shrugged. "In Hong Kong there was a great dignity, also some command. Since we came here you have turned into a peasant."

"One cannot be a successful dollar-girl if you are only a peasant."

"Why do you call yourself that always?"

"Because this is what I am, and you should remember it." This I said over my shoulder as I took the things into the fish-gamble. With a makeshift broom he had swept the floor and cleared away the broken crab claws and rotting lobster cages and swilled it down with sea-water, and it smelled fresh and salt clean.

"You see I have cleaned the place up?"

"I see it. It is good to be clean."

"Back home in San Francisco my mother was clean. She was so clean, though we lived in a tenement slum, you could lick milk off the floor. She had ten kids, I was the third son. And all the time I was growing up she was carrying one or the other, barging everybody around the kitchen with her stomach. She had them all in the hall, I remember. The neighbour women would come in and she would have those kids one after the other and never make a cry. You could have the street kids in and up and down the stairs and some might say, 'Where's your ma today?' and you would tell them her time was come and she was lying in the hall waiting for her baby, and they never said a thing. They never said a thing and they never heard a thing. My pa would come in from work and we would set the table for dinner and ma would still be in the hall, and not make a sound." He frowned at me. "You got women like that in China? Not a whisper, until that baby come, and then a caterwauling. But no sound from my ma. You could shiver with your finger up, and listen, and hear the neighbour women talking, and that was all." He grinned and sighed deep. "She was some woman."

"Is she still living?"

"Oh sure, she's still hitting up San Francisco. My pa's a drunk, so's Joe Kelly, his neighbour, with newsprint pasted over the windows and rubbish on the floors. Ain't no place to take a decent woman into, says my ma. But pastor comes regular to Number Ten."

"Pastor?"

"You call him priest? Pastor comes regular every Sunday week, half-past nine, for coffee and hamburgers."

"You going back there some day?" I asked.

"One day," he said. "One day when I clear myself of this little lot, I'm going back there. Right now I'm taking you down to the beach."

In the School, under the tutelage of the best espionage agents in the world, we are taught never to pursue the offered information, for this induces a cul-de-sac in the mind of the informer, a flare in the chemistry that will, given trust and time, unfold in detail a sequence of events. But time was not my ally. This is the fault of text-book espionage — nothing ever happens to waylay and divert the plan of the given example: things run far too smoothly. But given time and trust this man would tell me everything, if only to deliver himself of his tremendous crucifixion.

"You coming?" He was looking at me strangely.

For answer I shrieked and snatched at his hand, and we ran like animals over the sand dunes and along the beach with the sand-clods rising high behind us and falling in dull thuds. Into the cold tide-swim we went, now deeper, up to our ankles, running, running, and even when I lagged and shrieked for breath he dragged me on with pent joy. I saw the moon rising big in the stomach over the despondent mountains, with the crags sharp-razored against a cut-throat sky of blood. Bats swirled in from Taipa, the breakers thundered on to the beach, and I knew a cleanness with this black man that had no place in the tortured schemes of Old Man or the iniquitous traps of Kwan To Lin. Here walked no blind; no maimed by atomic light stood here where wave-lap sang and sea-lore spoke in China dusk. Here was peace, in this place of coldness where he had drawn me, and I heard nothing but his breathing, felt nothing but the warmth of him in that coldness, his fine body cording and tightening against me.

"You need me?"

He did not reply.

Standing there after the running it was like standing with some black shadow, for he had merged with darkness and only I was light. Against this shadow moved my hands, my hair, and these I saw. But the negro I did not see, and it was frightening. Nor did he speak as he untied the loops of my samfoo jacket and we laughed softly together, his teeth and eyes appearing like a vision from black velvet, as the loops drew tighter in his clumsy fingers. My hair he cherished, whispering against my face strange words out of his youth, perhaps, that I did not understand.

"You pay for me?" I asked.

"Don't you give nothin' free?"

"Not this, it is my trade."

It stilled him, and was meant to. It never fails to astonish me how lightly men treat the honour of asking a woman for love. From the cultured Kwan To Lin, with his trifles and whimsies, to the primitive lust of a black man on a jungle beach, they are all the same. For a moment I hated him, yet being desirous of him, loved him.

He said, "I do not want to buy you, Mei Kayling."

"I am a pataca woman. You want me, you pay for me, same as anybody else."

I could have wept for this man.

"Maybe I don't have enough money."

"The price is reasonable. One pataca for me, one for my uncle in Hong Kong, one for my grandmother back in China. Three patacas will not break you."

108

"I do not want to pay," he said.

"Soon you'll be saying you are falling in love with me."

"Maybe. I don't know; never had a woman before, the feeling's strange. I got over a thousand dollars in this hip pocket, but I want you free."

I said against his face, "They don't buy women like me down the *Beca da Roza*. You take me. You lose in me your fears. Perhaps you will even take me back to San Francisco?"

"Ah!"

"And show me to your mother, and even marry me — *Ai-yah!*" I shrieked.

He did not reply, he was kissing my face, my hair.

"You think the American Navy will stand in the way — you marrying a Chinese girl?"

I fought to keep calm; it was dreadfully hard to be calm at a time like this. There are no rules for this contingency, no suffering like this — the fight for coldness at a time of physical need. I said:

"What's bothering you?"

"Oh God, Kayling," he said.

I could tell of enchantment, but it was not this; of the fluttering bird in the hand or a spread-eagled assault on womanhood, but this was not so. It is a desperate shipwreck of love when you can remember it as nothing but a soothing joy: no elemental oneness, this, no sensuous stumble into love, yet a tumult for all the scheming, a gossamer fabric spun in starlight: a savage mating in a place of primitive wave-cry and fierce moonlight. His breath was sweet and clean; decency was on his tongue when he spoke to me. And when I opened my eyes wide to the man above me it was not Kwan, he who took and starved me, but the face of darkness, he who bestowed a rhythm of strength and beauty. In death or life, I did not know: I did not know the hour, the day, the year: neither the event that led to this, the patriotism that demanded it, the instructions to be obeyed. I knew only that I was at one with him, that his breath was mine, his blood, the

109

unfathomable concord of his presence. I knew not creed or colour, nor even the grotesque demand on dignity, for this copulation was surely invented by strange and abstract gods. Dying in the stuttering panic of his strength, with my heart and brain tuned into the honeying crucible where the wounding spear went deep in awful consecration, I called his name in echo, loud and clear, I think.

"*Negro!*"

I think I called his name, yet heard no sound. How quaint this loin-love, a sweeping up of the refuse of the body to meet the soul in ungovernable pace and pain. With clenched eyes I turned my face to the sea, knowing a revulsion, a growing sickness that I had used such beauty to seek another's torment. Now the lover gone amid his agony, I became his mother, whispering in Cantonese, my mother tongue, the words of consolation that he could never understand, and held his face to mine while his great body shook to the shuddering intakes of his breath. This unique and beautiful union between man and woman that, with compassion, transcends the biting lust: my first man, me his first woman, so negro said.

"Richard."

In the silence of gull-shrieks and wave-beat now; lying there with the weight of him moulding me in sand lithe and warm beneath me, I felt him listen to that echo of his name, and he drew from me with infinite gentleness and knelt beside me, smiling down.

"You said my name?"

In Cantonese I said, "I love you. It is wrong, for soon I will betray you, Negro — but I love you."

It delighted him and he clasped his hands. "What did you say?"

"It does not matter." I made to rise, but he slowly pushed me back into the sand and took strands of my hair in his fingers.

"Mei Kayling," he said.

Behind him the China moon flashed and beamed with her

110

skirt above her head in dreadful harlotry. And all the humour and delight of love danced attendance upon her from Jupiter to Mars and the Pleiades, their silken dresses gleaming red and silver, now gold and even green, streaking from the jungles of the earth to the caverns of the sky where gods made love, like this. The man above me spoke more, but I did not listen. The guttural noises that compounded into words held no place for me in this new paradise of peace. Here on a bleached shore I lay in elemental sleep, amid the dangling fish-bones of the gamble traps, the broken claws of crab and lobster and all the weed and putrid dereliction of the sea.

"Mei Kayling!"

I did not move as his arms went about me, but closed my eyes in Chinese prayer for this. And past the shadow of his cheek, a curve of tense muscle above the stretched sinews of his neck, I saw green lights beam from the eyes of the dead mare's skull on the pole, and the beach was scalded by a sudden wind from the sea, blowing typhoon hot from Taipa and the China islands of the sun. Brine bit this wind, stinging the face, the sea drove green in mounting rollers, streaming up the beach great foaming fingers to claw us into its thunder; now swimming about us in little eddies, caressing to my shoulders, unravelling and pulling out my hair over the sand. I opened my eyes to this new phenomenon, and saw by my hand the starved cormorant crouching for a friend, his beady eyes winking in the flash of the moon. I reached out, unseen, and swept him into the warmth of me, and there in the crook of my arm he lay, his feathers ruffling against my breast.

The man smiled and rose, standing above me.

Later, still naked, we went back to the fish-gamble. I walked behind the negro with the cormorant held against my throat. We did not speak.

111

CHAPTER TWELVE

In the morning I awoke to bright sunlight and the imperious cawing of gulls sitting in a white string on the ridge of the gamble. After a night of storm the wind of the sea was as cooling as wine, the sky a saucer of varnished blue, and night-dew hung spit-bobs from the drooling vetch-grass, the peroxide hair of the beach. The negro slept in black desolation, arms flung out, fists clenched, like a man running. Going down to the sea I there washed and did my toilet and returned with wild flowers, which are ketch-pan, the yellow idols of the sun. Love-making brings hunger, and I was aching for food, so while he slept I lit a fire on the sands so that he would not be disturbed, and on this I boiled rice and shrimpy big-boy tail-waggers, each one of which I kissed before killing and boiling, as I had done when young. And a Chinese patrol-boat from the Pearl River delta saw the smoke of my fire and came into the bay with foam on his snout all busy-body, and I braced my feet in the sand and flung rocks at him and cursed him in Cantonese, calling him mother of a pig and a dog's bastard until he turned in a welter of white wool, his prow racing east. With the rice snow-white and steaming in the pan and the shrimpies golden I went to the door of the gamble and shouted at the man, and he awoke in starts and stumbles, staring about him.

"Macau," I said, "Mei Kayling, to whom you make love, rice and tail-waggers, the sea is warm. It is a beautiful day!"

"Don't you put clothes on?"

"If you wish."

He rose, stretching to his great height. "Don't you bother," he said. "Never known anything more beautiful, Kayling, than being awakened that way."

"You wash and bathe and come to breakfast?"

He rubbed his stubbled chin. "Reckon I need a shave."

I squatted by the fire, keeping the rice hot and white for him, watching him swimming, and I cupped my chin in my hands, still watching as he wandered up the beach towards me with his indolent, native grace.

He ate in silence, black moodily, tearing the coarse bread between his strong white teeth.

"Today we must fish deep out," I said. "This is not really flounder-time, and the big rock bass make north for the China run this time of year. Only grovellers and tidlets for the purse-seiners we shall find in the surf, and these will not feed a belly your size."

"Last night I dreamed of you," he said at the bread.

I pointed. "Out there, beyond the China Islands, there is a ledge of thirty fathoms. See, I have kept some live-bait swimming, poor things. These we will bait down to eighteen, perhaps twenty feet, and the bass we shall catch will last two days, even in your teeth."

"You are strange and beautiful," he said.

When he had finished I gathered the bowls with studied disassociation. I did not eat this breakfast; for me it was starve, my mother advised, since there is a greater fear of conceiving if the child immediately has something to feed upon. Squatting in the tide-swill I washed his bowls, this time with samfoo trousers on, the legs turned up, decent, because I was his wife. He joined me, his shadow etched black on the rippled sand.

"How many men you know?"

"I would rather not discuss this," I replied.

He shook his head. "The way you act I don't think you've known so many."

"How can you be judge if you say I was your first?"

"A man can tell."

There was golden weed in the sea, long tubes of sea-flora with surf-anemones on the ends, bright pink and red. Among this I spread my fingers and formed a web of roots and posies, diamond glistening in the sunlight and tinkling with salt so that you could almost hear them singing.

113

The negro rose, drawing me up against him. "What do you feel for the men you take?"

His tone, his manner brought to me an anger. He was inducing an emotion in me which I did not want. He was bringing out of the routine of espionage a beauty I did not wish to feel. I turned away from him.

"You have not paid me," I said.

"It is terrible that you should want to be paid." Catching my hand he turned me back to him. "Need this be so? Now that I am with you and will take you away with me?"

I did not reply to this, so he said with great simplicity, "Kayling, I will give you all my money, I will not even touch you, if you will let me love you free."

"You put too much store on love. Later, when you are back in San Francisco you will meet a lovely coloured girl, and you will marry her, then you will forget about Mei Kayling, the Hongkongese."

"But you are here," he said, "and she is in San Francisco."

I laughed, and he laughed with me, our mood changing. We held each other, laughing stupidly, each new ring of laughter exalting the infection, and in the end we were clinging to each other, shouting with laughter, and the gulls wheeled above us cawing with curiosity, most perturbed at the stupid humans; it was all a little ridiculous.

"Come fishing now? Do not let us be stupid! Before the sun comes high, or we shall burn."

"*Hei up*, away!" He seized the prow of the save-life sampan and heaved at it, and I ran to help him, and we strained and skidded until the sand shrieked and the sampan ran into the shallows, batting and spraying at the breakers. We ran. Behind us, skimming over the surf, came the cormorant with hoarse cries. The sampan slid on the breast of the sea; the morning turned on its tap of summer, the sky glowed with vicious light. And the negro took the oars and drove us hard beyond Koho Point and into Shui-Tao, the Great West channel where the flounders dozed and the big bass played with the sea-cockles of Hirs. I lazed in the stern, then flung off my samfoo and baked in heat to the waist, and the cormorant perched on my thigh fighting for balance as the sampan rolled and plunged. Beyond us, dim with spray, the palácio houses of the rich grinned like false teeth along the *Praia Grande*.

"Fish, fish, *fish!*" I kissed the cormorant and threw him high, and he took up on a crest and sailed above us, swallowing hard on the ring, then dived, his skinny body, neck craned, plummeting without a splash. And came up almost instantly, beak stretched wide, body vertical as he fought the ring. The negro shouted with delight and swung the prow. Reaching down, I snatched the cormorant and thieved him, and the fish somersaulted on to the boards and flapped and thumped.

"Again!"

Again the cormorant dived and came up with a rock bass, floundering away with it for safety, so I threw back my hair and dived and got him, turning him in my arms, forcing him to disgorge the bass, then I slackened the ring and swam back to the gunwale and there watched him diving and eating his fill. Above me, elbow on the prow, the negro watched me. Like a black octopus he lay there, his hand on my shoulder, he who held the secrets of Kwangtung.

"I love you," he said.

This I pretended not to hear, for it is a thing any woman would care to hear twice. The sampan sprayed foam, the swell hit her along her shanks; below me as I trod water I saw the coral beds of Hirs; above me light burned brown.

"Mei Kayling. . . ."

Reaching down, he caught me under the arms and hauled me aboard, sitting me before him like a child: it was an astonishing show of strength.

"You hear me say I loved you?"

"Yes."

He took my hands in his. "You're not going back to the bars, Kayling. When the *Euranus* sails, you come too?"

"To South America? How can this be?"

I thought: yes, you are in love with me. Soon, in return for this love, I will leave you in the fish-gamble on some pretext and go to the steps of the Goddess Ama temple and see Old Man. Old Man, because he knows his women, will again convince me of the necessity of handing you back alive; and then, later, when he has got me safely in Macau, he will take the ferry to Coloane and cross the trail by my mother's grave, and seeing you on the beach below he will say, "Why, down there is Kayling's coloured man who primed the war-head that blinded Kwangtung," and he will kill you. The moment I am in Macau, Old Man will kill you.

It was dreadful to hear him telling me of his love while I was planning to betray him. I said lightly:

"But I have heard all this before. Many Americans married Chinese girls and gave them American nationality. But they didn't take them to New York or Boston, they took them out to the west to the Grandpappy farms. And there was Grandma and the family sitting with their feet up on the ranch, and the Chinese girls cooking and sweating for ten or fifteen, counting farm labourers. This I heard. It is better in the bars."

"Let me persuade you."

Later, when the sun came high, we pulled the sampan into the lee of Water Island where great trees, riven by the China coast typhoons, hung in green bounty over the swimming creek, and there he made love to me in the sensuous drowse of afternoon, amid blue-bottle hum and waving bindweed, and the sands below the sampan where no man had trod billowing in bucking shapes of green with a flash of mother-of-pearl.

And this fine loving was watched by the cormorant called Joe. Perched on the gunwale of the sampan he watched in statuesque blackness, not a single feather ruffling in his blank astonishment, and we kissed under the beady stare of his eyes.

"Joe is looking," I said.

"Please do not look," said the negro over his shoulder.

"This is impossible. Is there no privacy?"

"One would think that you did not mate also?"

"Or is it envy that makes you stare so hard?"

"It is envy," said the negro. "The woman in my arms is more beautiful than a skinny old hen cormorant."

"Fish, fish, *fish*!"

"Away, you peeping-Tom. Away!"

Reaching up with my toe I pushed him neatly off the gunwale, and he fell in a floundering splash to come up streaming with a fish in his beak.

"Mei Kayling," said the man above me.

"*Ah!*"

Joe choked the flounder down in gurgles and fell to staring again, but I did not care.

"Mei Kayling, you are strange and wonderful, and I am in love with you. You hear that, Joe Cormorant? Be witness to this, that I am in love with Mei Kayling."

I said, "But how can I love you back if you are always running?"

"What would you have me do?"

"Stop running away. Tell me," I said, "why do you run so hard?"

He kissed my lips and brine was on the tip of my tongue.

"Perhaps if I tell you that you will hate me."

"How could I hate you when I hold you within me, like this – but closer in my heart?"

"Because you are Chinese. How strange! In this light your hair is golden, yet at the roots it is black. Why is this?"

"Because I dye my hair to make me Chinese, but the scalp is stained for ever."

"It is so beautiful. Why do this?"

"Nationality is important," I said. "Look, see my body. It is coffee-coloured – you see this? Yet my hair is fair. Do you know something? Were I to make you a child it might be brown, or even the colour of a dove. And the second child I

117

would bear you would be true Chinese: black hair, slanted eyes, the nose broad and beautiful, like yours."

"It would come from you, Kayling. Only this is important."

I did not reply to this. To speak at that moment would have transgressed the sweet perfection of the day beset by sun and waves, and love. Lying here with him, his brain and soul enmeshed with mine, a single word might have sullied the grandeur, for tomorrow this black body might be dead. The cormorant watched, his gaze uncanny, his unblinking stare a condemnation; he made obscene the rhythmic pulse of sea, wind, humans.

"Kayling, do not heed him."

Later we forgave him, and tired of watching humans love without the solace of a cormorant mate he dived, and we gripped the gunwale with our hands and stared like awed children as his brown body, neck extended to the rending flash, rushed in distorted shapes of refraction through the translucent haze of island dunes and jungle green. Tired of watching the cormorant fish, we lazed, drank gorgeous coca-cola in scarlet bubbling, eyes clenched to the sun; and loved again into the China dusk while eddies of gold swept in fragrant from Taipa. The tide of the Pearl River slapped and thumped. I saw in a rift of the negro's hair the dancing wavelets of the Great Channel as the sea swam in, and the hovering birds, their cries faint in the man's breathing, and heard his pent tumult — he the captive now, for men in strength are weakest. I held him, and said:

"Because I am Chinese, I should hate you? Why?"

"It does not matter."

"But it matters to me, if I am to live with you."

He said, "Those who died, those who were blinded in Kwangtung, these are your people. Because of this one day you will hate me."

"Because you were on the ship that did this?"

He drew away, staring. "You know this?"

"I guessed it. You are a very important deserter."

He lay back. "At night I dream of it. It was like any other trial. We had done it a hundred times...." He paused, adding softly, "But how did you know it was a missile from a ship?"

"Yesterday I learned it at the ferry. It is in the Chinese newspapers. A missile came from a destroyer of the *Hunter* class, it said: the Americans have admitted it."

"My God!"

"They admitted everything," I continued. "They are paying enormous money into the Bank of China. It was a long article. They said it was a war practice, that the rocket was not directionalised, or something. The drill war-head had been changed by somebody, it said. You were silly to run."

He answered fiercely, "If I had not deserted they would have pinned it on to me." He made a fist of his hand and bit at the knuckles in agony. "Somebody used me. I was the armament sergeant. I stored the war-heads, I held the key." He turned upon me. "It was just too easy. I clamped on the projector beam. It was painted yellow, like all drill projectors. I've never seen a live war-head and projector base, for they are red. I just sat on the deck the day before we left port, and screwed them on while the rocket stood in the slides."

I said, "It is all too technical and I do not know what it means."

"It means that they used me to arm a drill rocket — somebody high up working through either Kurtz or Hamer — it could have been one of another half-dozen guys aboard; they used me because I'm coloured."

"To take the blame at the inquiry?"

He said in his throat, "Either Kurtz or Hamer...."

"Who are these men?"

He wiped his sweating face. "Hamer was First Lieutenant Armaments. He retired from the Navy about a month ago. We had him during Vietnam, he was a real bastard."

"And the other man?"

"Kurtz?" He sighed. "He replaced Hamer. For an officer

119

in charge of ship munitions he was a dream. He didn't even care where the bomb bay was – left everything to me."

"Where is he now?"

"I suppose he's under arrest."

"And Hamer?"

This turned him. "Oh, Hamer was clever. He got out in time. Like me. If they ever get me they're getting me dead. A minute after the thing exploded they had me under guard – like as if it was all arranged."

"How did you escape?"

He grinned in recollection. "They only had two guys with me – they should have made it six. After I'd put them out I slipped down a rope and swam – we were in from Taiwan then, anchored off Green Island. It was night. The tide took me down through the harbour and I got ashore at North Point. By morning I was in Kowloon City, the rest you know."

I said, though it was a lie, "In the papers it says that they've arrested Kurtz and Hamer. Did you expect this?"

"Kurtz maybe, but Hamer too?"

"So the newspaper said."

"They've got it wrong. Kurtz, maybe, because he was aboard, but not Hamer – Hamer was important, he had connections."

"You know about him?"

"I know more about him than's healthy. I made it my business. After I'd done naval service, I used to tell myself, I'm slipping down to Pittsburgh to see to that bastard. He led me the life of a dog."

"Perhaps he did," I replied. "But that's no proof that he changed live equipment with drill equipment just to get you into trouble."

"But he was responsible – you understand that?" He brought his clenched fist down on the gunwale. "Hamer saw this stuff aboard, he signed for it, and he's responsible."

"But surely Kurtz took it over – wasn't he officer in charge?"

"Kurtz was a nice guy, but he was a dud. He gave me the keys, and I took over. Anyway, I was the fitter, not Kurtz. I armed the head and the projector, and that's why they put me under guard." He paused, staring at me. "Why am I telling you all this?"

"Because you've got to tell somebody. I'm not very intelligent, but it is good to tell somebody. Please go on."

He said, "I'll never forget that rocket blowing. It was a shambles. The trouble was the casualties, and this wasted time, otherwise they could have got the anti-missile device going and diverted it out to sea. A lieutenant and a marine sergeant were standing beside the projector when it went. The officer was blinded, the sergeant died of burns. I was off duty — below in my bunk — but Kurtz was up on deck. I heard the speakers going and the red warning ringing. Everybody was shouting for the anti-flight crew and the radar crew — you understand — it was a drill launching and nothing was supposed to fire. People weren't even in position; the moment the Rocket Layer switched on his circuit the bloody thing went. And even when it blasted off nobody realised it was armed with an atomic war-head, and it wasn't supposed to be directionalised." He added bitterly, "But it was, of course. It was live, it was fused, it was calibrated and laid and it was rocketed. Everything was right for war. By the time they got it on the radar it was over Kwangtung, above the Chung Mountains. The radar followed it down, and the calmest man on the ship was the captain. Maybe there had been a launching and firing mistake, but it was just another drill rocket dropping in a bunch of mountains. . . ."

"And then?" I asked.

He shut his eyes. "Then we saw the flash. It wasn't an ordinary flash. Even from a distance of eighty miles it was the brightest flash I've ever seen — a ball of neon-lights hanging in the sky for five or six seconds, then the mushroom came rolling up."

"An atomic bomb."

"Small, only about two megatons. It was for shore attack,

121

in support of large-scale landings by infantry. No fall-out, no radiation; an eyesight bomb."

I said, "How terrible."

"Everything went mad then. The navy's all right while things are going right; when they go wrong it's a bloody kindergarten. Everybody was shouting for circuit suspension and radio silence, the wounded were screaming. Operations got the explosion area located. It was on the edge of the mountains, north of Canton, near a village called Hoon."

"Hoon?"

"About six miles north-east of Canton. But it was Canton they were worried about – populated area. We broke radio silence to Hong Kong and asked for instructions, calling it a ship-board accident, and we were told to report back there immediately. On the way to harbour they took me under guard."

I scarcely heard his last words. I was thinking that it was imperative to report this to Old Man at once. Kwan must be kept informed. I believed every word the negro said. The man Hamer, I thought, appeared of the greatest interest. If the launching was not official – and, from what I had heard, the official American circles were as horrified as the Chinese – then Hamer would have to be found and interrogated. The negro said:

"You're sure they have picked up Hamer?"

"It said so in the newspaper."

"Queer," he replied abstractedly. "I should have thought he was too hard to find."

Lightly, I replied, "You mean he's in hiding for some reason or other?"

"You might call it that. But I can pick up Hamer any time I like."

I did not ask more. There is a limit to the extent one can go when you are acting the role of a Hong Kong dollar-girl with relatives in China.

His money, I knew, was in his hip pocket; in that wallet there might be other information.

If the information was in the negro's head, then it would be up to Old Man.

A slow disgust was sweeping over me. It grew in immensity, developing almost to a physical sickness. I hated myself.

Above the creek a heron was flying. The tide was sweeping in now. We took the sampan down the Great Channel and drove it for the sand of Coloane. Leaping out, I ran, the cormorant flying ahead of me in swoops, now wheeling above us. The negro followed, shouting hoarsely, and I heard his feet plodding in the sand behind me. Catching me, he swung me down at the foot of the gamble, kissing my lips.

"It does not matter, all the time I have you," he said.

I covered his lips, turning away my face.

"Mei Kayling!"

I struggled away from him and went into the mat-shed.

It was no use. I could not continue with this. It was up to Old Man.

The negro entered and drew me into his arms.

"Don't do that, don't ever leave me," he said.

CHAPTER THIRTEEN

There was a fuss and fume in me to get to Old Man.

China, as Kwan once said to me, demands the whole, not a partial, loyalty, not a half subservience. In the death by suicide of Peng Teng we see this epitomised; either one is with the Cultural Revolution or one is against it. Weakness in the individual is the strength of the mass: only the mass is important. Strength in the individual is self-will, and self-will brings in its wake self-interest. This is but a play to ego: is bourgeois and decadent, a breeding ground of revisionism at a time of anti-revisionist purity. It diverts the Marxist-Leninist line, it traduces the thoughts and aims of our beloved Chairman Mao.

It is disgusting to be at odds with oneself.

123

I spat at the name of this negro.

The heart is but a valvular instrument that can be found in an ox or a pig. How can emotion stem from an instrument which is but a munching, pumping machine fulfilling its function like the lower jaw of a cow?

I hated this negro as an enemy of the Cultural Revolution.

This I remembered as he kissed me; with my fine left hand I expertly took his wallet and slipped it into the pocket of my samfoo jacket.

"Do not be long, Kayling," he said.

As I left him to go to the ferry he sat cross-legged on the sand below the fish-gamble, and the cormorant he called Joe strutted at his feet. Rather like an overgrown piccaninny he looked, sitting there, round-eyed, black-faced. It was suddenly very easy to leave him. In his hands he held a little flask of whisky, the western escape from reality, his cul-de-sac of hypnosis. Whisky plus the total acceptance of a ruling class authority, Kwan once said, will be the ultimate downfall of western civilization. His name, he said, was Richard Wain: it was a delightful name by any standards, it rolled like honey off a tongue. To me his name was Negro. Only the guiltless are entitled to a name.

"Goodbye, my darling," I said.

I had timed it so that the ferry was waiting, and I went aboard and sat amid the sweating, steaming labourers of the Coloane waterfront. Strangely, the sweating Chinese exude no smell: this is because they eat little meat and few fats and drink little milk, which is the food of babies. Europeans smell very badly, and for many reasons. One, a fat-rolled woman in lace-frilled white, was sitting in the prow. In the stern I wrinkled my nose, and the Chinese wives smiled with me. I stared through the launch window at the rolling sea and the billowing wash-day clouds flying above Taipa, listened to the thumping roar of the diesel. Negro would be a little drunk by now, I thought, his feet in the tide. Old Man would be sitting on the steps of the Goddess Ama, awaiting me.

This is exactly what he was doing, as if he had been there for weeks: a maggoty crow of a creature, eyes heavily lidded against the sun.

"This is astonishing," he began, rising. "Will you believe it, I have this moment arrived – we must be psychic."

"I trust it is the only thing we have in common," I said.

"Your mood is poor?"

"My mood is excellent. It is the company I keep that I find depressing."

"You refer to the negro?"

"I refer to you."

He said with delightful grace, "You are intolerant of my seniority, Kayling. The law in China demands respect for the aged; it used to be a good law."

"It used to be a good China," I said. "Here is the negro's wallet."

I ought to have been ashamed. It was an appalling show of temperament, and one which, even a week ago, would have sent me back to China for thought-rehabilitation. I walked away from the temple, and Old Man, with a fine display of creaks and groans, raised himself and hobbled after me.

"The hotel Caravella," he said. "And try not to act like a Mandarin actress."

"I am sorry," I replied.

"You will do more. You will officially apologise."

He pulled gently at his goatie beard, his old face collapsing into a myriad ingratiating smiles; he bowed to the passers-by.

I thought it unnecessarily dangerous to bring Lin Ho, my espionage mother, to Macau at a time like this, and said so; Old Man shrugged me aside and called the bell captain, who showed me to my room. Lin Ho was awaiting me, and she had come in style: beautifully dressed in a gold cheongsam, she was standing before the mirror as I entered. One would have been forgiven for wondering who was mother and who was daughter. I stood before her in my drab samfoo.

"Well, well," she said at the mirror, "we do look in-conspicuous."

"I have got the information you want, Lin Ho."

"You were a long time doing it." She patted her hair; it was done most beautifully in a chignon style; mine was in dish rags around my face and neck. "There are passable ways of extracting information — actually I examined yours from a patrol boat off Great Channel. It was extremely interesting."

"I am glad it entertained you," I replied. "When one gets older one has to resort to the gun."

"Which your negro would not have enjoyed quite as much. Well, report."

"I report to Old Man, not to you."

"I see." She plied lipstick with an expert hand. Behind her I stripped off my samfoo jacket and pulled my hair to my waist. Beyond the lattice window I could see the fish-flounders slicing the hills of Taipa stark against a sky of russet gold. I thought: soon he would wind the winch and bring the nets in on the gamble, and leap down in the surf with the foam streaming white on his black shoulders, his white-palmed hands flashing at the fish. And shriek like a delighted child if he found one, calling me, and I would not be there. Later he would sleep, and in the morning look along the sands, and I would not come. Then he would climb the hill near my mother's grave and look towards Coloane ferry. Later still he would find his wallet gone, and he would understand.

I washed my hair, I bathed. When I was dressed Lin Ho spoke on the telephone and Old Man came in, closing and locking the door.

"Report," he said.

I sat on the bed, Lin Ho sat by the window with an air of indifference.

I began, "Let this be clear. I work for Kwan To Lin, not for you. I did not ask for the assistance of this woman, and I do not do so now. I insist that she is removed during this report. If you do not agree I shall immediately return to Hong Kong and report officially to Kwan."

"Delightful," said Old Man.

I walked around the room with pent rage. "I mean it. I shall not report to you."

Old Man sighed deep. "I am deeply obliged to the Central Committee for this assignment. They serve me strange parcels — a disaffected negro and two bitchy women." His fist hit the table. "Do you realise the dangers, the loss in time while you two quarrel?"

"There is a simple remedy," I said. "Remove her."

Lin Ho rose, smiling down at him. "And what about the negro?"

He said, "Tell me one thing, Kayling, has he given you all his information?"

I nodded.

Lin Ho said, "Then surely he will no longer be needed?"

"If he has done this he cannot be returned to the American authorities," replied Old Man. "Within an hour they will learn that he has been in our hands, and we shall be involved." He eyed me.

"It is essential that they do not know that we are involved," said Lin Ho.

I was trembling, and they both knew it. The trembling flew to my fingers and I locked them together, turning away to the window.

"Shall I go tonight?" asked Lin Ho.

"If you please," said Old Man.

She smiled at me. "This will be a pleasure." Taking a little automatic from her bag, she snapped its magazine into position.

Old Man rose. "After Kayling makes her report. That will bring darkness — it is safer done by darkness." He belched and patted his stomach. "And it relieves me of a distasteful business. I could kill Americans in tens of thousands, but, never individually. Individually likeable, they are collectively an abomination; no nation has the right to be so schizophrenic. Killing individual Americans is to end their native charm: this I should find far too distressing. So you, Lin Ho, will have to kill this negro."

Old Man, by some Chinese magic, had the ability to vanish or appear at the lift of a finger. When I came out into the fairy-lit garden of the Caravella he was already seated at a table overlooking the *Praia Grande*. Above him the bauhinia trees were etched in blackness against a round China moon; below him waves rolled in crashes to the black shore. He rose, bowing.

I said, "I am sorry about my behaviour. I do not like that woman. I think it is quite stupid that she should come here."

"So do I. Kwan sent her. Were I twenty years younger there might be certain advantages. Please do not distress yourself."

He poured us Casalhino wine. Sipping mine, I watched him, wondering about the negro. From my window I had watched the road. I had not seen Lin Ho leave the Caravella. Old Man sipped and tasted, his eyes vacant. To me he was the complete enigma, something that had stepped out of an ancient dynasty into the intrigue and espionage of modern China, and it seemed a little ludicrous that Peking, with its insistence on a sharp division between the old and new, should perpetrate this sort of cloak and dagger Fu Manchu character as seen by the west. No doubt Old Man paid his way with his efficiency and ruthlessness — cruelty unmatched was his reputation, a violence made fragrant by his old world charm.

"This is excellent wine," he said.

"Why has Lin Ho come here?"

He shrugged. "Mere routine. Agent spies on agent, it is a tender business; probably a good idea to keep us all in order. Her next move, strangely enough, will depend entirely on your report."

"You have read the negro's wallet?" I asked.

"It is a mine of information, though we knew most of it before."

The waiter came. Old Man ordered fried rice, sweet and sour pork and boiled garoupa. He also ordered a great display of wine, most of which was from Portugal and therefore free at the Caravella. Old Man's income must have been tremendous, yet it was said in Peking circles that he knew the date on every coin in his pocket.

"Now then," he said.

"I would much rather give a written report."

"Quite impossible."

"Who will take it to Peking?"

"Lin Ho. She is nearest — frankly, I cannot spare the time."

"Why cannot I take it myself?"

"Because Kwan is expecting you in Hong Kong tomorrow."

I said, "Listen to me. It is essential that only the facts be reported. Embellishment of the facts, the slightest colouring of reported events, could produce the most damning circumstantial evidence, and I do not trust Lin Ho to convey them accurately."

"The Party does. You make the report. Leave it to the Committee to worry about embellishment."

The food came. He began to eat with noisy relish. I said:

"The destroyer *Hunter* is a unit of the America Seventh Fleet based on Taiwan. On the eleventh of June she left Hong Kong and sailed north as far as Quemoy. There was nothing unusual in this, it was a normal patrol. Soon after midday it was decided aboard this destroyer to carry out a routine drill — the arming of a rocket with its projectile base and nuclear war-head, its mock firing and its tracking by the ship's radar system."

He appeared to have fallen asleep. With chop-sticks poised he was slumped over his bowl. The coloured umbrellas of the terrace billowed suddenly in a wind from the sea, a night-bird shrieked from the banyan trees.

"Please continue," he said.

"According to the negro he fitted both the rocket projector

129

and the drill war-head in the slides on the day before the ship left port. He drew the equipment from the armament store, he checked it himself, and fitted it."

"Under supervision?"

"There was an officer in charge, but he seems to have left things to the negro."

"Go on."

"The crew were called for the drill. Actually, the negro was below decks when this happened. And immediately the rocket-layer switched on the circuit for the mock firing, the rocket discharged."

"It projected."

"It projected and flew. There was immediate panic. Proof that it was never meant to fire is there — one man was killed, another blinded — they were standing too close to the launcher-slides."

"What happened then?" Cheeks bulging, he munched.

"Then there was panic. The anti-flight crew were called and positioned, the radar brought to bear. When the rocket was detected it was flying north-east of Canton."

"Then it was directionalised for that purpose."

"According to the negro it was not directionalised — this is the whole point. And even when they failed to destroy it in flight nobody was particularly worried. They believed they had projected a dud. Only when they saw the flash did they realise that they had launched an atomic bomb."

"And then?"

"They broke radio silence and contacted Hong Kong; they were recalled instantly."

Old Man nodded. "It was as I thought. The negro was used as a tool."

"He was arrested on the voyage back. He knew he would be the whipping-boy. He slipped the guards and deserted — he swam down from Green Island to North Point; that's how he got into Kowloon City."

"Were the dummies and live heads kept together?"

"In completely different parts of the ship."

130

"Who held the keys of the magazine?"

"The captain. But for occasions of trials he handed them over to the armaments officer, a Lieutenant Kurtz. . . ."

"Who handed them over to the negro."

"How did you know?" I asked.

"We have checked Kurtz. He is quite innocent and was probably tricked. What about this man Hamer?"

I smiled. Old Man said:

"We have efficient contacts also. Did the negro speak of Hamer? His address is in his wallet."

I said, "It seems that he had a personal appointment in Pittsburgh with Hamer."

"And intended to fulfil it the moment he was given the opportunity."

"He thinks Hamer framed him, as he calls it."

Old Man sighed. "Everybody frames everybody else in America, it seems." He held up a piece of soiled paper, and read, 'Lieutenant John Hamer, New York. Address 147 East Twenty-second Street, Pittsburgh.' Yes, this is sufficient confirmation. We both adopt completely different paths, we both finish at exactly the same cross-roads. From now our paths diverge. You go west, Mei Kayling, I go east. The situation is important enough for me to report to Peking in person."

"And the negro?" I took a deep breath.

Old Man rose. "Your report makes it clear that he is the most important piece of evidence. He will be interrogated on Coloane."

I could have shouted with relief, and to cover this emotion picked up my glass of Casalhino, sipping it and staring at nothing while Old Man watched me.

"Where is Pak Lin Ho, then?" I asked.

He smiled. "Now on her way to Coloane. Tomorrow she will interrogate him by gunboat patrol — he will not be harmed, his existence is precious — and he is best left where he is."

"And I am going to Hong Kong, you say?"

"Kwan To Lin awaits you. He is most impatient for your return. Further instructions you will receive from him. Tomorrow I will give you your passport, suitably endorsed to get you through the Customs. You will be on the twelve-ten hydrofoil; a car will meet you at the Hong Kong jetty at one o'clock, and a room is booked for you at the Mandarin Hotel."

"We are going up in the world," I said.

"It might need watching. Kwan has probably booked the room next door." He rose. "You must be short of clothes and travelling bags?"

"I own what I stand up in, by courtesy of Lin Ho."

He put a roll of Macau notes in my hand. "Right, spend freely — enjoy yourself. It is going to be a different life from this moment. Spend, spend, it will gladden your woman's heart."

"That will not be difficult."

He threw up his hands. "Become the lady of good standing, groom yourself for western company. You are beautiful, you speak well, but you lack many of the pampered graces essential to the woman-about-town. On Coloane you were a dollar-girl: be a woman again."

I replied, "Do not blame me, Old Man, for lack of womanly grace — blame the drill parades, the celebration squares, the rifle, the bayonet — blame the Party. You cannot have a head for war and utter femininity."

"I don't know, Kayling, you did a surprisingly good job on the negro. And Kwan, unless my opinion fails me completely, will ask you to do a similar job on this man Hamer."

"In America?"

"In Pittsburgh, to be precise."

Bowing, he left me.

CHAPTER FOURTEEN

I often wondered if Old Man did the passports himself. Lin Ho had once remarked that with his ability as a forger he could command the highest fees in the world of criminal philately. Certainly the beaming smiles I handed out to the young Portuguese Customs officials appeared unnecessary. The sun was bright, the air sweet and clean as I pushed my way through the queue and heaved my suitcase along the Hong Kong Praya.

Kwan was awaiting me in a Mercedes taxi, sitting at the back with his legs crossed, a cigarette in his mouth, exuding the air of one not to be tampered with.

"You are late."

I lowered the suitcase with a sigh. "This is becoming a habit. I came when I was instructed, and the hydrofoil is exactly on time."

"One day late."

I said, "Perhaps you could have done a quicker job on the negro."

It was a stupid remark, and I instantly regretted it.

"I was really considering the job he did on you. Bundling up and down the beach. Idyllic, no doubt, but you should have had him interrogated."

"That is happening now."

"Not before time."

I said, still on the pavement, "It would be rather nice if I could come in."

He swung the taxi door wide and slid over to make room for me.

"The policy was not mine, you know," I said. "No doubt you could have interpreted it better."

"There you have me at a physical disadvantage."

He was infuriating. Within seconds he was having upon me the same devastating effect of frustrated anger. The taxi edged into a shunting, honking stream of chromium and paint, driving before it a wedge of protesting pedestrian and bicycle traffic. Never had I seen so many people on a road: you could have walked on their heads between the ferry and the Hilton.

"The population has risen," I said.

Kwan replied, "It is a panic exodus. Taiwan is making the most of it, of course. Their foreign agents are reporting the possibility of further large-scale attacks, and hinting in press and on radio that it will be American."

"And threat of invasion?"

"Hints, hints – Chiang Kai-shek and Son sabre-rattling, though the Americans have made it perfectly clear that they would never support Taiwan militantly."

"It is a tremendous pity," I said. "It is my undying ambition to see Americans swarming over our mainland."

He sent me a penetrating glance. Kwan's perceptions were best when he initiated the moves; the task of his listener was to remain passively intelligent.

Against the shuddering, protesting background of samfoo humanity I took the opportunity to examine Kwan in profile. His good looks, I decided, were deserting him. Espionage and women were taking their toll. It was whispered that he was a heroin addict, taking the drug to extend coition, which, according to the sniggers of the class-rooms, was nothing to do with the moon, sun or zodiac. No doubt the Politburo knew all about Kwan and his paramours: at this rate he would soon be back in Peking, replaced by the brilliant Ku Ata. Meanwhile he was not to be taken lightly, and I was not the least surprised when he said:

"I have completed the dossier on this man Hamer."

"You don't waste much time."

"University of Pittsburgh, athlete, executive – in a bank, I believe, but this is obscure. Now aged thirty-nine, married with one child, a girl. Captured north of Seoul, spent ten months in a North Korean camp."

"But you have more?"

"A little," he replied, "not much. After all, I'm working from a distance of thousands of miles."

"And this is all foreign agency?"

"Surprisingly, much of it is local. Hamer is well known in certain circles. A nation of the tongue and fist, Kayling. The very fact that they nurture free speech and copulation gives the rest of the world an enviable advantage. It will lose them the last war of all."

"Philosophy will not get us any nearer Hamer," I said.

"Ah, but it will. Philosophy and self-analysis have got China where she is today. And the absence of these qualities has landed America in the mess she is in today. To know Hamer one must study America, and Freud. For instance, this nation has progressed industrially and economically faster than any on earth, but, having no ability to self-analyse, she has been mutilated culturally. For the bar-room brawls of the Middle West we can substitute her lust for modern violence; for the atrocities perpetrated on her unfortunate Indians we can substitute her atrocities in Vietnam. It is a pattern of behaviour unchanged for two hundred years. Violent, cruel, talkative, this is America. With a minimum of risk it is also Hamer."

I sighed, untouched. It was all really quite excellent, coming as it did from Kwan To Lin.

In the astonishing opulence of a Peak tea-room we padded on the tapestries of Tientsin amid the nasal phonographics of scurrying American tourists: up the winding stairs now and into the gilt decor of the gorgeous tea-room and we sat, Kwan and I, in an architectural madness while sloe-eyed waiters in bum-freezing jackets drifted in absolute servitude from table to table under the bulbous domes and tinsel decoration of a nightmare called creative genius.

"Ask for a prostitute and they send you an architect," said Kwan.

A waiter brought the tea and poured while we watched profoundly: the pouring of tea such as this is a balm to the disquieted mind. I closed my eyes to the scented steam while the *Tea of the Mountain Clouds above Honan* stained amber in the brimming bowl. No sound but the faint hiss-sigh of agony; one can feel the frantic scalding of the egg-shell china. The waiter left us, sending one glorious look of adolescent appraisal at me over his shoulder. Kwan said:

"You have the most profound effect upon males."

"It is a matter of training."

"But you'll have to be at your best for Hamer."

I sipped my tea. "Which is another way of telling me I'm off to Pittsburgh?"

Two young people came in, English by their looks and accent, and they sat in the chairs nearby. The boy was brawny handsome, his head black curls; the girl was aesthetically beautiful, and jubilant, her laughter ringing out in a blessed oblivion of youth and love. I thought she was absolutely delightful.

"It is an avenue of exploration," said Kwan.

"I beg your pardon?"

He said, "It is necessary to prove, and beyond doubt, that the firing of the armed rocket was intentional, and that behind this intention was official American action."

"A White House decision?"

"Not necessarily — an *official* decision, one backed by elements of the Pentagon."

"I take it that Hamer is in possession of such facts?"

"Probably not. But if we can find who was employing Hamer, who, in turn, used the negro for his ends, we might prove or disprove this."

"I might fail in this," I said.

"The possibility is unthinkable."

I looked at Kwan. The complete professional: one who was hardly capable of cutting his own throat to save mine. He said now:

"It will be difficult, make no mistake. Hamer has been investigated. We have been through his house, his office, his yacht on the Monongahela River; on the face of it he is as

136

innocent as the doves who undoubtedly sent him to do the work of a hawk."

"He lives with his wife in Pittsburgh?"

"Fortunately for you – separated; this makes him accessible."

I said, "It is an astonishing world. On the intrigue of a few men world murder arrives. America is the brigand of the peace. And China so badly needs another thirty years of peace."

"Not at the expense of honour."

"But, Kwan, if the Kwangtung disaster was accidental . . .?"

"Accidental or intentional, we should go to war."

I said, "I do not believe this. Remember the words of Chairman Mao – '. . . This is an era of peace. Wood cuts soil in the plough, iron cuts wood; fire forges iron and water quenches fire. This is an era of water, and water breeds tranquillity, which is peace!' "

"You make it sound beautiful," he whispered. "But I don't believe it."

I said with great sincerity, "Kwan, peace is his policy. In the past few years we have made two hundred and thirty-eight official protests to America, ranging from the violation of air space above the Gulf of Haiphong to atrocities in Vietnam. Can't you see – this is sabre rattling. Amid a Cultural Revolution of this magnitude, how can China make war?"

"Don't put your life on it, Kayling."

I said, getting up, "China has other gambles when it comes to my life."

I knew, of course, that when night came Kwan would try to make love to me. Never had the opportunity or location been so tempting, and a woman grows more enchanting with the passage of time. But I knew I should reject him, and for Kwan this would be a devastating disappointment, a repeat of history. It was all a little boring now. To please him I

137

might have acquiesced, which is a delightful word for smoothing the sheets of a bed, but, as the Chinese ancients say, it is a happier state to sleep with a dead pig than an uncomplying woman. Strangely, most women give themselves to men not for a personal gratification but for pity, the very human desire to be of service. The poets lace this wine with a very heady emotion, baiting their literary hooks with an eating female greed, but this is only the projection of their own ecstatic urge of sex: in fact it is nothing like this. The gratification of desire is so easily replaced by love, the emotion I felt for the negro. I would have given to him, to ease him. For love is mere simplicity, humility, kindness: all these I felt for this negro. None I felt for Kwan whose need was not particular. Kwan ate, slept, shaved, took a woman. A smile, a drink and thirty dollars would supply all the requirements of the external appendages of his stomach; internally, it could be satisfied by a meal at Maxim's for another fifty. No, it was not quite so easy; not now, Kwan.

"I am sorry," I said at my bedroom door, pulling my dressing-gown closer about me.

The expression he wore now I had seen before on a man at the 'House Full' sign at the Chinese opera. Men are strictly limited, I find, in their store of expressions in such circumstances.

"But this is ridiculous, it is the second time!"

"It will become even more ridiculous if I call the manager," I said.

A year ago I would not have contemplated this refusal. One said yes to Kwan To Lin out of sheer idolatry. Now it was merely funny, and I badly wanted to giggle.

I said, "If you're a bit short I can lend you thirty dollars."

"Do not be disgusting."

"And don't you be a nuisance, Kwan. Go to bed."

Closing the door in his face I leaned against it. Air moved from the ceiling-fan, touching my face with fingers of ice; the air-conditioning was on full. Moderating it, I went to the window and leaned on the sill, staring out on to a blazing

Hong Kong, but I did not see the great city in all its complexity of mood, its beauty or its stark tragedy. Instead, I was examining a phenomenon. Until this moment I had not considered that my brutal rejection of Kwan was based on anything more than a desire to retain my personal integrity and put him in his place. Now I realised, with passionate force, that it was based on something infinitely greater; a reason that snatched me up with unassailable beauty and power; an emotion that transcended in height and strength anything I had experienced before.

Somewhere in the garish, brutal splendour of Hong Kong a clock struck midnight. I drew myself up, put my hands in my hair and willed myself through the alleys of starred darkness to a place of white moonlight and wave-crash. And I knew myself suddenly in exultation. I understood this unfathomable emotion.

I did not want another man to touch me: only this negro, on Coloane.

Remembering Kwan's embrace, his searching lips, I knew a revulsion in his warm, animal presence.

Remembering Coloane, I slowly went to my knees by the window and there hugged myself, trembling.

Only once before in my life have I wept like this – before the sniggers of the children of Hoon, standing in the market-place, aged twelve, albino.

Afro-Asian concord, the Marxists would have called this phenomenon, the inevitable proletarian reaction, kind for kind: a psychological interplay of emotion natural to kinship. Or even a unity through love of the exploited masses of the earth.

But I wept on, calling his name, biting my fingers.

He was probably asleep in the fish-gamble, I reflected: dreaming of me, the trash pataca woman from Wanchai or the red light quarter of Macau down the *Beca da Roza*, the prostitute who took his wallet.

I wept on. It was unforgivable self-pity.

139

CHAPTER FIFTEEN

At breakfast next morning I gathered the impression that Kwan was a little jaded. The gentlest enquiry enlisted that he had gone to bed early and slept badly, a distinct victory for the moderates. But my bed was not as virtuous as Kwan's, for I had slept with the negro. I slept with him in the fish-gamble, listening to his breathing; ran with him on the sands of Deep Channel when the tide was spent, and made love to him in the seaweed bucking sampan on a cobalt-crested sea.

"You are no longer with me," said Kwan.

"I am sorry."

He stirred his coffee abstractedly, a habit he owed to the Americans he was pledged to destroy, and in the ornate room the early guests wallowed in English porridge and festooned their fingers with thin, brown toast, a machine-gun crispy fare without which the Stock Exchange, the casinos of the west, would run below par; and with prinked little fingers sipped their coloured fruit juices in dilution of the alcoholic injuries of the night before. The Japanese marmaladed and pouted in stumbling rushes of conversation, or sat in the inscrutable transistorised daze of the forlorn millionaire; the Chinese shovelled and gasped, shouting joyously at their pampered, red-clawed mistresses and wives. It was exciting, and I felt splendid, actually winking at Kwan over my tea-bowl, and winked again at his scowl. Glowering, he slapped butter on little rice-cakes and munched at nothing with the vacancy of a Sinkiang cow. I spoke twice and he did not reply. Old Man once explained it. Repression in the venal functions of the male, he said, brings in its wake a most stilted conversation.

"And what happens today?" I asked.

"You are taking things far too lightly."

"Who can blame me? A week from now I'll probably be dead."

"Most probably."

For people fighting on the same side, it was an astonishing situation.

I thought, watching him: Kwan To Lin, I was a fool to love you. You are not even handsome. In darkness, in the role of courtly wooer, you are at your best. But here, Kwan, in daylight, under the unsparing radiance of a Hong Kong morning, you are very dull. Given my way, I would place on you the white smile of my Coloane negro, whom I betrayed. I would raise you nine inches in height, barter your woman's arms for corded strength. I would paint black glitter on your body and move you in sweat and cat-like grace, take from your throat the light sounds and make them bass. Simplicity for you next, and you would let fall the intellectual asides and planned understatements. I closed my eyes, seeing in their lidded blackness an island glittering with sun, the hills of China savaging a varnished sky; great cumulus clouds lumbering across the caverns above Coloane. Down by the fish-gamble he would be waiting, and I should not come.

"White, two-timing, Cantonese *bitch*," I whispered.

As if called, Kwan frowned at me over his chop-sticks.

I smiled to charm him.

"Now," said Kwan, "you will listen most attentively."

We were in the foyer of the Mandarin. Espionage, written popularly, is executed in remote country houses and cellars, but it is not more efficient because of this. In the Chinese version we usually put things underground by the expedient of mixing it openly with the mass where its identity is lost. Because it was useless to hide Kwan's identity, for instance, we exposed it, including his weaknesses which his enemies knew – his love of women. Counter-espionage is always off its guard when an agent is seen with a paramour in public. New China might be prim, its new-found purity the belly-laugh of the west whose virtue has gone for ever, but China is a modern when it comes to the spy. Here was Kwan's latest, listening dutifully to Kwan in the sighs of his cheque book. The panic and chase for the woman of Wanchai would begin tomorrow when I disappeared; by then I should take some following.

"Ku Ata arrived in New York this morning," said Kwan. "Lum is due there within two days; he is going by sea."

"There is a reason for this timing?"

"None which may concern you."

I said, "But Ku Ata will support me?"

"There is no support this time, Kayling. This time you are on your own."

"Then why talk to me of Ku Ata and Lum?"

"It will become relevant, in due course."

I wished he would come to the point. This was the trouble with Kwan. Like Old Man he induced a sense of the dramatic, he set his stage and air of mystery, and I wanted nothing of it. I said:

"Tell me about Hamer."

"Let me tell you a little, first, about Ku Ata."

The Colonials were coming in off the street for morning coffee amid their plunder of everything Chinese from Pakhoi to Taku Bar; women mostly, cosily meeting in their class strata for their coffee-jabbers, apparently about one another by the sound of it, while beyond the plate-glass window, where stood a giant Sikh, the burned and blinded of Kwangtung stumbled in the gutters. Kwan was talking about the famous Ku Ata, but I was not really listening, since he was practically text-book in the School of Espionage.

In his time Ku Ata had been China's secret idol. Indeed, he was once head of D.I.3, the service branch of the Politburo, but fell from grace by open criticism of the Hundred Flowers speech, being accused of reactionary views directly opposed by dialectical materialism, and only his brilliance in the espionage and atomic field put him back into official favour.

Kwan said, "He exists chiefly, I suppose, as a man whom China cannot do without."

Ku Ata, born in Hankow of a Chinese mother, was the product of an enemy during China's agony. His father was Japanese. While impossibly young he graduated with honours in atomic physics at Peking University, and was one of the team of scientists at Lop Nor who exploded China's first atomic bomb. Yet his true love was espionage, and in an age of specialists Ku Ata discovered an affinity between atomic physics and espionage.

Now I began to wonder in which capacity Ku Ata was visiting New York.

"And Lum?" I asked.

Strangely, I could never get Kwan to discuss the fanatical Lum, the Red Guard leader who would deem it a privilege to die for China, such paranoiac loyalty being a little oafish, to Kwan To Lin's tasteful mind. One thing was sure – this was one who would vapourise his body to advance his country another six-inch step along the path of Mao's Cultural Revolution. It was said that Lum took his orders direct from the powerful Lin Piao, but I never had the proof of this. Now Kwan said:

"The man Hamer, the one who stands accused by your negro, is well known to us. If this is the same Hamer as we have on our files – and this is one of the points you must clarify – then he once was, if he is not now, an official American agent. Understand this, Kayling. Peking is demanding two points of clarification in this assignment. First, as I have said, proof beyond possibility of doubt that the man called Hamer whom we have on our files is the Lieutenant Hamer who once served aboard the destroyer with your negro. Secondly, absolute proof that he used the negro to fire an atomic missile, and that this was an action planned either within the Pentagon itself or by a body of leadership closely related to the American Government."

"The manner of proof required?"

"A photograph of the man Hamer and a recorded statement by Hamer that he actually planned the explosion and left the negro to execute it."

143

I said, "Very reasonable. If I leave in the morning I'll be back by Wednesday."

"Do not be facetious."

"You are asking the impossible."

Kwan shrugged. "If you think that we had better get another woman down from Peking."

I said, "Do I get any support at all?"

"Support will arrive when you least expect it, or if you are desperate. Remember this."

"You won't enlarge on that?"

He shook his head. I said, "Where is this Hamer?"

"Pittsburgh. You will not be entirely alone. You will be met in New York by a freelance agent named Jan Yentin, an excellent man. He is based on Miami, but will escort you to Pittsburgh and instruct you in Hamer's whereabouts. Yentin will book you into the Roosevelt Hotel, Pittsburgh, under your European passport name of May Warren. You are a traveller in ladies' fashions; Yentin is your American representative. You yourself are actually based on Tokyo, so you will fly Mandarin jet at midday tomorrow from Kai Tak to Japan. The Americans are particularly sensitive towards civilian passengers arriving in the States direct from Hong Kong, so it is safer for you to be based on Tokyo."

"Yentin identification, please."

Kwan nodded. "Here is a photograph – keep it. Yentin is about thirty-nine. Born in Amsterdam of Dutch parents, both died in a German concentration camp. Yentin was also an inmate. The number 2155 is tattooed on his left forearm, probably indistinct now since it was done when he was a child. He has a heavy Dutch accent, and will speak in French."

"And if I succeed in getting a recorded statement from Hamer and a photograph, how do I channel them to you?"

"You give them to Yentin. He will channel them. He will supply you with a suitable tape-recorder and camera – you merely hand everything back to him."

"Hamer identification, please," I said.

"At this stage the less you know about Hamer from me the

144

better. Yentin will brief you down to the last detail, he knows a lot about the man – much more than I do – but there is one thing that I do know and you will not like it."

Kwan lit a cigarette and exhaled smoke lazily at the ceiling. "Hamer has a record, with women." He smiled thinly. "The very nature of espionage leaves time on a man's hands; this being so, his mind naturally turns to trifles."

"It is a poor excuse, Kwan."

"But forgivable. The women are inclined to be beautiful, which makes it no easier. But Hamer's record holds little of romance. An agent's background sometimes determines his attitude to counter-espionage. Twice, in Korea, Hamer knew torture, though the Federals did all they could to cloak the truth. Hamer slipped – twice – and in each case it was a woman who trapped him. You remember Dorothy Ming?"

Dorothy Ming, once a most promising agent of the new Guard, was a text-book copy of the perfect female in espionage. Her best work was on the Indian frontier, when she brought back a complete disposition of Indian defences after a ten-day holiday in Karachi. In view of this success she was assigned to the Delon Group, a quasi-French Communist agency working within the United States based on Baltimore. After the death of their president, Dorothy Ming became their leader through the sheer brilliance of her espionage. A steady flow of information came into Peking; coup succeeded coup and the American C.I.A. was continuously outwitted. The F.B.I. demanded an inquiry into the leakage, and C.I.A. put their best counter-agents to track down every member of the Delon Group, Hamer being assigned to the Baltimore area. Within a week of Hamer's arrival in Baltimore the body of Dorothy Ming was found in a deserted farmhouse beyond the city confines. She had been brutally and sadistically murdered, the manner of her death being too horrible for print.

"I remember Dorothy Ming," I said.

"Then remember Hamer. Treat him with care. When you sup with the devil you need a long spoon."

145

"And assuming I get this information, how do I return to China?"

Kwan replied, "This also will become clear to you."

I nearly told him that I was becoming impatient of his profound secrecy; that if I was going to take my chance with a sadist like Hamer I had a right to know more than a bare outline. It was all right for him, sitting here in the security of the Mandarin making his asides and innuendos, but it was an impoverished sort of contribution to the job in hand. Yet, strangely, the very hint of danger was bringing me to a trembling excitement. Inwardly terrified, I was yet externally cool. That Kwan was watching me intently I had no doubt. And I had no doubt either that the faintest show of trepidation would land me back in Peking and bring another in my place. I heard myself say:

"And Lin Ho – what part does she play?"

"Lin Ho?" Kwan glanced at his watch. "With any degree of luck she is already in Pittsburgh – if she managed to get the right 'plane. Unlike you, Kayling, she doesn't have the advantage of an escort. Incidentally, she has met Yentin and thoroughly approves of his ability."

"Air passage?"

"This has been booked through to Pittsburgh. The ticket is in your passport."

"Money?"

"I will give you two hundred American dollars."

"Is that enough?"

"Yentin will give you more if you need it; it is unwise to carry too much. Old Man has handled your entry visa, he prides himself on these – do not worry on this score, concern yourself with the man Hamer."

I said, "Answer me something. What are my chances of coming back?"

"Your return is a certainty or I would not be sending you."

"The truth, Kwan."

He examined the end of his cigarette. "The truth? About ten to one against."

146

I took a deep breath. "Peking accepts such appalling odds?"

"Presumably. I have absolute clearance on the assignment."

I got up. The foyer was thinning. Beyond the window the street was brilliant with sunshine, the harbour deep blue and crested. Racing wallah-wallahs bucked and rolled in foam, the ferries grunted and swayed, and farther, beyond Kowloon, the hills of China raked at a summer sky. I said:

"Surely a country like ours expects better odds than ten to one? This information is vital to China. Upon this mission depends the fate of countless generations – it could be nuclear war or peace."

He was instantly agitated, and rose beside me. "Oh no, Kayling – we are at serious cross-purposes. You asked me my opinion of your chance of coming back, not the odds against China getting the information she requires. She will get that right enough – the thought of failure doesn't occur to me."

"But I may not return, that is it?"

"That is precisely it. You are still prepared to go?"

A sickness rose in my throat and I swallowed it down.

"Of course."

Kwan was reflective then, rubbing the side of his nose. "One must be a realist in this game. It is this man Hamer, you see. He changes the odds. There was Dorothy Ming, Jenny Lee-shan, Han Moy-tor and about three others – all good agents, but none returned from Hamer."

I could have done without this. Undoubtedly Kwan was enjoying himself. This was the personal intrigue of espionage that had no place in the rule book. I had to smile despite myself. There are penalties for virtue that cannot be envisaged. I said:

"There are compensations, Kwan, in dying for China."

He smiled at me. "But not in the way one might have to die."

147

CHAPTER SIXTEEN

It was often said in Social Security circles in Peking that Old Man, as head of Movement in the Far East, had missed his vocation in life. Under different circumstances, working for the west, he would have dominated the highest executive ranks in the travel agency profession, except that, on the side, he might also have forged the cheques. Now I was learning the measure of his genius, for I swept through officialdom at Hong Kong where things were understandably touchy at the moment, was first through the passport check at Tokyo, and hustled into an enormous Pan-American jet with four minutes to spare. Sitting there forty thousand feet above the Pacific bound for New York, I was so impressed by the clockwork precision of Old Man's genius that I was initially unaware of the impending crisis in my life: that at the end of this journey the man Hamer would be waiting, up-river from Pittsburgh, and that it was ten to one against my ever coming back. Even when I had left Hong Kong two days ago, roaring into the sky above Kai Tak with the distant land of China rolling to the horizon far below me, it had not occurred to me that I might be looking upon my country for the last time.

Now an impression of isolation and loneliness struck me with crucifying force.

The 'plane droned on. San Francisco came and went, and I thought of the negro of Coloane; of the tenement slum where you could lick milk off the floor, of the nine brothers and sisters, the drunken Pa with Joe Kelly, his neighbour, and the pastor coming regular to Number Ten. The wheel of my life seemed to have turned full circle. As a dot in the sky I was the invisible link between Coloane and San Francisco, the sunlit island of the east and the tenement of the west, the kiss between mother and son. I wondered if the negro was dead. The thought bowed my head and screwed up my hands, and the man in the next seat peered at me above the pince-nez glasses. I wondered if Lin Ho had killed him or if Old Man had taken him into China. And I made a vow that, if I could beat the ten to one odds and return to China, I would go to Coloane and seek the negro.

And then, once again, I remembered Hamer, and I felt unequal and defenceless. It was a travesty of the teaching that I should feel like this, I thought: pegged, spread-eagled, a bait to the tiger. A *bait*. The thought brought me upright in the seat. It was impossible. Kwan might do this to me, but never China.

"You all right, miss?"

It was the man beside me. He was old. Weariness lay in his eyes behind the thick lenses, but his face was kind. His cent, I remembered later, was heavy American.

"Your first flight?" he asked.

I nodded, though it was a lie. Anything to get rid of him.

He smiled. "I do this trip every month. Business, you know — Tokyo and New York, New York and Tokyo. Pan-American — like a 'bus. Do not be afraid."

A bait. The man spoke again, but I did not hear him. If this was so, even with the odds at ten to one, I would get out. I would get out of America and back into China. In Hong Kong, in Macau, in Peking — wherever he might be, I would find the truth. And if he had sent me as bait for Hamer, I would put a knife in Kwan. I was trembling, screwing my hands in my lap. The old man beside me patted my fingers.

"Another ten minutes and we'll be back on terra firma, child. Do not be afraid." It was strange, this kindness, coming from an American.

In tyre-whine and wing-sag we touched down, rose, touched again and slid in rumbling, staccato speed along the tarmac. The astonishing terminal building of Kennedy stretched out beside us; the big jet ambled to a halt. Now the descent to earth. The man Yentin was standing near the barrier.

"Miss Warren?"

"I am Miss Warren."

"Yentin." He put out his hand. "Good trip?"

"Excellent," I said. His photograph, in my handbag, was an exact likeness.

Yentin lifted my suitcase, saying in French, "I hoped you'd be on this flight. The Polav Boutique is showing in Pittsburgh at six-thirty – the 'plane leaves for Pittsburgh in half-an-hour. If you're lucky with the Customs and Immigrations we might make it."

"We will try," I said.

"Is this all the luggage you've got?"

I nodded, adding, "They didn't mention this particular show in Tokyo."

"Probably didn't know about it." His eyes drifted around. "It's new as a fashion house, new management, new designers."

"The sooner the better," I said.

He actually winked. It was a trifle slap-dash, but I thought it charming.

He talked in gushes, this one, and in broken French with a heavy accent, the undertones guttural. He was a big man with a power that came out and struck you in the face, and handsome; in his late thirties, I supposed, as Kwan had said. My confidence was returning. It is the actor in the agent that is always most impressive, and his gaiety was infectious after the dedicated Kwan. We caught the 'plane to Pittsburgh with a minute to spare; with only six other passengers aboard Yentin took the opportunity to talk.

"You have been in touch with Kwan?" I asked.

"Through Lin Ho," he replied.

"Pak Lin Ho – she is in Pittsburgh?"

"She arrived there yesterday."

We sat in silence, staring down at the rolling farmlands of Pennsylvania.

"Proof of identity?" asked Yentin with a smile.

I gave him my passport, being a little astonished that he had not so far asked for this.

"And proof of yours?" I said.

For answer he rolled up his left shirt-sleeve. His forearm bore the mark of a faint tattoo. He smiled, saying:

"2155, though with the naked eye the number is hardly discernible. Photographed and blown up it is very clear."

"Concentration camp?"

"Belsen. I was only ten years old. My parents were Dutch Resistance."

"They died in Belsen Camp?"

"This is the belief. Actually they died on the way to Belsen. A friend of my mother was in the same truck, and she adopted me on the spot."

"It was a terrible beginning," I said.

He rolled down his sleeve and fixed the cuff-link. "To be tattooed with a number is convenient at times like this. For more serious identification it can bring you to an ignominious end."

"It is a dirty business, and no more than we deserve."

He shrugged. "Perhaps. Anyway, I'm getting out, after this Hamer business."

I looked about me. True, nobody was within ear-shot and we could not be seen, but I was a little surprised that he should mention Hamer's name at such a time. This was careless, and I was not used to carelessness. Kwan would have been appalled by such a breach of regulations. I said:

"You have located him?"

Yentin lit a cigar and glanced around. It was the first time I had seen him show apprehension at the possibility of being overheard. Espionage in the west, I was concluding, was not the blank-faced variety which we promoted in the east. He said, "Hamer's not so difficult to find. He's got a yacht on the Monongahela, a beach-house in Miami and a flat in New York – he's usually at one of the three."

"Right now?" I asked.

He stretched himself with a sort of cosy weariness. "Right now he's on the Monongahela River, that's why we're going to Pittsburgh."

"Describe him, Yentin."

I thought he was going to sleep. It was very disconcerting. Yentin said:

"Young — about forty, dark, very handsome. A powerful man — I'd not like to tackle him. He was a sort of *enfant terrible* of the C.I.A. He's unorthodox — he gets his information in ways that keep me awake at night — and in the end the C.I.A. sacked him. Do you know he's a sadist?"

"They mentioned this."

"With a particular liking for unprotected women?" He eyed me.

"They mentioned this, also."

There was something disgusting about it. By the very nature of the profession one expects no mercy: one does not expect a continuous play on the terror, either. Yet I had never failed to notice this degree of smooth contentment that enwrapped the informant of such terror. And it seemed to me, sitting there, that Yentin was rather like Kwan in this respect. He was watching me, appearing a little surprised when I said:

"So far Hamer's had it all his own way. When it comes to sadism we're not uninformed in the East. Where was he between June the tenth and the twenty-first, have you discovered?"

"I beg your pardon?"

I said, "Between the tenth and twenty-first of June — was he out of the States?"

"As far as I know he was in Miami between May and the beginning of July."

I asked, "You have his record?"

"In detail."

"You will let me see this?"

"If you think it will help."

I said, "Mr Yentin, it is not what I think will help, it is what I ought to know. If I ask where Hamer was between certain dates it is up to you to tell me, through the record, to my satisfaction."

"Dear me, we are going to have an informative time."

"When we understand each other better you will find me enjoyable to work with. You have the information, the background location, you have been able to assess the opportunities. It is your job to tell me everything you know — I should not have to probe for information."

"That is what they pay me for."

"And highly, Mr. Yentin. Now then. Where was Hamer between those dates?"

He replied, a little bored, "If we are going to become administrative at the drop of a hat I will refer you to the file index." He lay back in his seat and tipped his hat over his eyes. "For that, Miss Warren, you will have to wait until we get to Pittsburgh."

I stared down at the flowing land of Pennsylvania. I was not very impressed with the efficiency of Jan Yentin, upon whose efficiency my life depended. I was not impressed with Chinese counter-espionage in America, come to that. The Japanese were superlative, of course, people like Ku Ata appearing once or twice in a generation. Yentin was actually snoring in starts and fumbles; it was almost unbelievable. I had the impression that when we reached Pittsburgh he would telephone Hamer on the Monongahela River and ask him if he was available.

It was dusk by the time we touched down at Pittsburgh and dark when we reached the Roosevelt Hotel. Yentin remained in the back of the taxi as I got out.

"I'll 'phone you," he said. Somebody slammed the door and I walked away without a backward glance. It was an inauspicious beginning. At least he had booked me in. A tired-looking porter took me up to the sixth floor in a lift, his sallow face stricken with ten thousand comings and goings of no significance, but on the landing he suddenly turned and said:

"Did they tell you there's a lady waiting in your room, ma'am?"

I shook my head.

There was no time for surmise, for the door was opened.

Lin Ho was sitting on the bed. Her hair, I instantly noticed, was dyed fair, the colour of mine. I tipped the porter, locked the door.

"You are not surprised?" asked Lin Ho. She rose with her usual grace and wandered about.

"After that man Yentin nothing surprises me." This I said in Chinese.

"The room is safe, I've been over every inch of it," she said.

I put down my suitcase. "What are you doing here?"

"Didn't Kwan tell you I was in Pittsburgh?"

"He did, but he also assured me that I should get no support from you."

"There is no support, my dear, for what you're up to."

This I ignored. It seemed to be developing into a game of who could frighten whom, and I was far too tired. I said, sitting down:

"Then what are you doing here?"

"Now, there you have it, Mei Kayling. I ought to have the perfect answer to that, and yet I have not. You know your English literature?"

I was wishing her to the devil. My head was splitting. What with the mental indolence of Yentin, the threat of Hamer, and the autocratic attitude of this one, it was becoming too much.

"Your Shakespeare? Such brilliance, remember? It is only the scholar Mei Kayling who can say three plays by heart, eh? But Dickens, my dear? In a race with tigers one must keep up with the tigers. He actually visited here – Dickens, you know."

I said, "You are talking nonsense. What do you want of me?"

She spread her hands. "*A Tale of Two Cities?*"

"What of it?"

"The infamous, noble Sidney Carton – remember?"

154

I stood looking at her. She said, smiling, "He who died for his friend?"

"What are you trying to say, Lin Ho?"

"That I am about to die for you."

She was enjoying it, the perfect actress. "My hair, you see, is fair. In looks and figure we are much the same. Seventeen years between us can be salvaged with a little paint and powder. I wear passably well, considering I have played the part of your mother. What do you think of the idea?"

I said, "Lin Ho, I am tired. Say what you have to and finish with it."

"It is very simple — haven't you guessed? Come now, if you are to handle the tiger in Hamer you will have to do better than this. Peking want you back, didn't you know? Mind you, it could be for interrogation, or it could be for adulation. It rather depends, I believe, on how you do with Hamer. International politics are notoriously sly."

"And where do you fit into this?" I asked.

"I am of a lower value — the great expendable. When you get all you want from Hamer — and you will not fail in this — there will be a hue and cry. You may have got into America with Old Man's genius, but it will be much more difficult getting out."

"Go on," I said.

Her eyes were bright, her face the colour of alabaster. With her hair dyed golden she looked impossibly young. Her legs were long and shapely, the black dress she wore enhanced the beauty of her figure. She snapped her fingers, saying, "So you fly off to Tokyo. I book a ticket to Hong Kong." She smiled. "Hong Kong is where all agents book to when they want to be caught."

"This is official?"

"It is, according to Kwan."

"What happens to you then?"

She walked about with accentuated gestures. "Then I become Mei Kayling, Red Guard. I carry a duplicate of your passport, I am still young enough to stand the first scrutinies.

155

I am an actress, they will find me most convincing. By the time they know I'm a fake you should be very far away."

"It will take five days at least," I said.

"That is the time I am supposed to last – five days. It will be practically a record, they tell me. Now what do you think of that, Kayling?"

"I would do the same for you."

"Make no mistake, I'm not doing it for you."

"Do not blame me," I said. "Blame Kwan, the Politburo, but I had no hand in it, so do not blame me."

She said, screwing at her fingers, "I have two children. True, the girl is a dud, but the boy is at university, for he is brilliant. Don't you think it all a little sad?"

To my astonishment she began to cry in gasps and wheezes. I could hardly credit it. One might cry for love of country, for the death of Chairman Mao, even for the death of a parent. It is inconceivable that one should cry for oneself. I said curtly, "Come, this is quite ridiculous. You have been psychologically prepared for this event, it is a normal part of the curriculum. Please try to pull yourself together."

"It is my son," she said, and wept on, spluttering into a cage of fingers. It was quite dreadful that she should stand there crying like a child, with tuneless sounds of grief. The mascara was staining her face, her lipstick was smudged: grief can be obscene. Vaguely I wondered how she would stand up to the beatings of the interrogation, and if she would last the vital five days I needed to get away. On this performance she was certainly casting doubt.

"Kwan ordered this hunt-the-hare?" I asked.

"It was arranged even before you left Hoon."

"And you have met Yentin?"

She was wiping her eyes with her hands. "In New York."

"He knows of the intention to get yourself arrested?"

"He probably organised it."

I walked about, hands clasped. She was probably right that this was organised weeks ago. This was the reason why they had taught her every fact of my existence and the fiction of my upbringing in Hong Kong and Macau. Strangely, I did not pity her. This was her role, that of the sacrificial goat. It could be a proud one, executed with dignity.

"Give me your tablets, Lin Ho."

She stared at me, her eyes opening wide in disbelief. I repeated:

"Your tablets. Give them to me."

Her handbag was on the bedside table. She moved instantly, but I was quicker, snatching it from her hands. She watched, trembling, as I opened her suicide kit, took out the suicide instants and replaced them with morphia. Her voice was shaking when she said, "What are you doing?"

"You are no good to China dead," I replied. "Anyone can die. You have got to last, understand? Double morphia, but stay alive."

"Yes, Kayling."

I snapped the handbag shut and gave it back to her. She took a step towards me, her hand out. "But what about you?" she asked.

"If I collect Hamer," I replied, "I'll have no need of morphia."

The telephone bell rang then, its note strident. We stared at it.

"Room 204?" It was Yentin's voice, speaking in French.

"Yes," I answered.

He said, "Speak, please."

I replied, "I will speak as clearly as I can, caller, this is not a very good line."

He grunted audibly, apparently satisfied with my intonation, and said:

"Listen intently. It will have to be tonight."

"That is impossible!"

"There is no choice. He is leaving for New York on the eight o'clock 'plane tomorrow."

"Delay him. I refuse to be rushed into this."

Lin Ho said swiftly, "Kayling, you will have to do it. . . ."

Yentin said, "Are you still there, caller?"

157

"I am still here."

"Who spoke to you then?"

"You should know, you met her in New York."

There was a pause while he took things more slowly. I was impressed. Yentin the indolent who was unpossessed of social graces was not the Yentin of the chase, apparently. Hamer was in sight now, and Yentin was going. Now he said crisply, "For God's sake understand. This may be the only chance we have. This is my area and you are under my command. Meet me outside the Duquesne Club at eight o'clock — the cab-driver will know it. And tell your friend to leave at once."

The receiver clicked, so I put it down. My hands were shaking. A moment before my fears had been blanketed by time. Days had stood between me and Hamer. I had no plan, either for attack or for retreat; I had not even prepared a mental brief. Lin Ho said smoothly:

"Trust Yentin, he is good. Yes, I know he looks lazy, but this is part of the spoof." She added, "And go now. Play it as it comes — you can do it. Sometimes it is better done quickly."

It was a complete reversal of her mood, an admirable show of control, of uplifting courage. She took her handbag from the table and threw her coat over her shoulders. At the door she asked, "You have your passport?"

I nodded.

"And I have yours," she said. "Everything is identical, except for the photograph. Old Man is a genius. Except for the age — even Old Man can't change that." She turned her profile to me, smiling. "How do I look? May Warren, nationality British, born of a Chinese mother, father English, a man of the sea. Raised in Hong Kong, working for the Chinese equivalent of the C.I.A." She made a charming gesture. "One is caught in the act — there is no possible reason for denying it. Only the age . . . this is the trouble. The age is the tell-tale. I am forty-one, and you are listed in their filing index as twenty-four."

"It will take them two hours to work that one out," I said.

"A blatant mistake – unforgivable. Somebody will be for the high jump." She smiled, adding, "Perhaps they will not notice. The first half-hour is bad, they tell me. After the first half-hour there shouldn't be much difference – facially, at least – between you and me."

I did not reply. At the time it appeared a pathetic attempt to induce sympathy. This was Lin Ho's fault, I reflected; her character at times was weak.

"Remember me," she said, and lifted my suitcase, "No – I take this one, these are the instructions. You take mine – there is nothing in it – it is down in the hall."

"Goodbye, Lin Ho," I said.

But she did not open the door. Lowering her voice to a whisper, she said, "And more instructions. Look out of the window and watch me leave. Do nothing until you see me go. Then, fifteen minutes later, leave for the meeting with Yentin."

I said, glancing at my watch, "That will make me nearly twenty minutes late."

"Exactly, and, although he doesn't know it, this will assist Yentin."

She softly closed the door. I waited, walking the room, then imperceptibly drew the curtains, looking down on to the dark street. After an interminable wait Lin Ho came out. It seemed strange that she should take so long to pick up a taxi. The taxi slid up to the foyer as she approached the kerb. A door swung open. Lin Ho got in and the cab roared away.

It was then that I noticed the glow of a cigarette from the opposite sidewalk. The glow moved and a man stepped into the street, staring after Lin Ho's taxi. Almost immediately a car stopped beside this man and he got into it. The car drove off south, the way Lin Ho had gone.

I was beginning to admire Jan Yentin.

Undoubtedly the man shadowing Lin Ho was F.B.I., now going in pursuit of Mei Kayling. The hare-hunt had begun. I looked at my watch.

It was five minutes to eight. Sighing, I sat down on the bed, to wait. Kwan's original conception, perhaps, but it was being executed by Jan Yentin.

It was really quite brilliant.

CHAPTER SEVENTEEN

Yentin was standing on the pavement near the Duquesne Club looking at the moon. I called to the cab-driver and he brought the car to a stop. Yentin got in beside me.

"Riverside," he said. "I'll tell you when to stop."

We did not speak. I was aching to tell him that it was almost impossible for me to approach a man like Hamer with hardly a moment's notice; that I had no distinct plan; that I needed time to orientate my senses to the new surroundings, to meet Hamer a couple of times informally, to get the feel of him. It was not just a matter of failure and dying in a way that would delight Hamer; repercussions were at stake that might hammer China into insignificance for the next hundred years. It began to rain, pelting on the windows of the cab as we sped on through neon-flash and beaming headlights, going down Duquesne towards the waterfront. Billows of mist swirled in from the fork of the Allegheny and Monongahela; masthead lights glowed red and green; Coal Hill and Washington Heights pulsated yellow tinsel, like fairy mountains. We crossed the bridge and hammered in wet swishes towards the far jetties. The cab stopped and Yentin paid the driver.

"You're going to get wet," said Yentin, and took my suitcase.

"Is it far? I'm in high heels," I replied.

"About a quarter of a mile."

We walked through the debris of the waterfront, where fingers of mist searched among the stored cargoes of the stack-yards; crates and boxes littered the way: steel wire ropes wound over the railway lines and loading-bays, glisten-

160

ing in the rain like varnished cobras. About half-a-mile up-river a warning light burned. Yentin stopped in the doorway of a deserted warehouse, and pointed.

"See that light?"

I wiped rain from my eyes, nodding.

"That's the barrier," he continued. "Do you see the tall masthead lights to the right of it? That's Hamer's yacht. He uses it when he comes to Pittsburgh. We go this way."

Turning, he led a path towards the river, and soon a charming little house-boat made shape through the mist. Yentin said:

"I booked this about a week back, to be near to Hamer. I've actually tapped his telephone extension, but it proved a waste of time. Tapping went out with the stone-age – all he uses the telephone for is dates." He took my hand and helped me along the house-boat gang-plank. "You've got competition. They come up this jetty from eight to midnight in all shapes and sizes."

I was sweating badly. It was a personal disability that had always plagued me in times of stress, and the more I worried about it the worse I sweated. Yentin unlocked the door of the house-boat and I went within; sweat formed in rivulets between my shoulders and ran in a stream down the middle of my back. Yentin said lightly, "You look cool enough, and with good reason. Hamer will be easier than you think. And you won't be alone in this, you know."

"I assumed that there would be no help, Yentin. I have not asked for any help."

Locking the door he went to a cocktail cabinet. "You'll have to have help. You can't just walk into his state-room and pick him off the shelf. Did Lin Ho get away all right?"

"About ten minutes before I left the Roosevelt."

He glanced at his watch. "That means she'll reach the airport at about eight-thirty. There's a 'plane for New York just after nine. Her shadow will advise her if she gets lost."

"Describe her shadow," I said.

He squinted at the light. "Tall, raw-boned, pretty dowdy."

"I saw this man," I said. "Tell him not to smoke in doorways, that cigarettes shine." I looked at Yentin. "F.B.I.?"

He nodded. His eyes, I noticed, were suddenly incredibly sad. "F.B.I.," he said. "I did it by an anonymous note – 'Chinese agent Mei Kayling leaving Roosevelt for airport at eight o'clock.'" He sighed. "Sometimes this business stinks."

"Do you think she'll last five days?" I asked.

"She'd better, or you won't get back to China."

I sat down in discomfort. My wet dress was sticking to the backs of my thighs, crowding me with a physical depression that enhanced my growing sense of disaster. Yentin was speaking, but I did not really hear him. All this was nothing like I had planned. The meeting with Hamer was to have been a slow progression of situation and circumstances that would culminate in a confrontation: I had begged of Kwan the opportunity to assimilate his characteristics over a reasonable period of time, and he had promised this. Now I was being bull-dozed into a head-on crash that would have as its reason some far-fetched fortuitous incident, and Hamer would hardly be such a fool as to fall for that. Next they would be wanting me to pull up my skirt on a public highway. I said to Yentin, "I have news for you, Jan. Ever since you telephoned I have been giving this careful thought. I am not seeing Hamer tonight. With or without support – by you or anyone else – I am not meeting Hamer under head-on conditions. I told Kwan that I need a fortnight and I demand a fortnight."

"And Lin Ho?"

"They will not arrest her until she books her 'plane ticket to Hong Kong."

"And Hamer?" He was watching me coolly. "If he leaves for New York tomorrow it might be months before he returns."

"Then I will meet him in New York. I will not be stampeded."

"Vietnam, Cuba? You don't know Hamer. A week from now he might be anywhere."

"You will not change my mind," I returned. "I am assessing this situation as I find it. Short of violence there is no chance of making Hamer speak, and I am not trained for this."

"I am," said Yentin.

His eyes were shining, I noticed, but this I had attributed to the drink. He appeared to me to be a compulsive drinker and I wondered if Kwan was completely informed of this. He rose, glass in hand, saying, "You are not alone in this, you know. You can shout your patriotism as loud as you like, but to some of us this is a profession, and it means money. I work for the highest bidder, and every pint of Hamer's blood is worth a thousand dollars."

"This is the trouble with the professional," I retorted. "If the price is right he mutilates his mother."

He leaned towards me, smiling down. "Ah, now we are getting it!"

I said, "The task was assigned to me, Jan, not to you. Kwan knew of Hamer's weakness for women before you knew of Hamer. The toughest doors in the world are opened by call girls. Hamer rings for a girl and I arrive."

"But this takes time, Kayling. My way is swift, and it is the only way."

I got up. He was probably right, I knew this. I think I had known right from the beginning that control and pain are the real ingredients of speed. Behind me Yentin was slopping whisky into a glass. I reflected that it mattered little how the information was obtained as long as China was served. Yentin would do the butchery and I should get the information; also, I would shoot Yentin. My hands closed on the tiny automatic in my handbag. I was beginning to like Jan Yentin and did not want to kill him, but it would be safer to do so. Yentin had a mouth. Whisky went in, information came out. A week from now, through counter-intelligence, he could be the enemy of China.

I said over my shoulder, "You are perfectly sure that Hamer is leaving first thing tomorrow?"

"Perfectly. It is routine information, this never fails." Jan drank his whisky, smiling. Behind him were crimson curtains, presumably leading to a bedroom: it was a charming little room, tastefully furnished in a Dutch Renaissance style, so typical of Yentin's European charm. It had the hand of a woman about it. Vaguely, and completely out of context with the situation, I began to wonder if he was married. Now he said:

"Tell me what you want."

I replied, "The Central Committee wants a recorded or signed statement from Hamer of his part in the Kwangtung disaster. They want to know the people or party behind him — whether they were mere fascists, adventurers, men representing business interests, such as arms manufacturers, or men with influence in the House of Representatives."

"Or even in the Pentagon."

"Or even in the Pentagon," I repeated. "The Central Committee demands the identity of any movement or institution employing Hamer; they demand to know the role of a negro sailor named Richard Wain and a Lieutenant Kurtz, both of whom were aboard the destroyer *Hunter* when the atomic missile was fired. In addition they wish to know if the captain of this ship was involved with the firing. And, lastly, they require a photograph of Hamer for positive identification of a man on the files of the Chinese Central Intelligence."

"And punishment of Hamer? Don't they demand this, too?"

"If he is proved guilty, death by shooting."

"At the hand of Mei Kayling?"

I nodded, saying, "Kwan told me that you would give me a camera and a tape-recorder."

"Both are ready, do not worry. You will watch me work?"

"It is my duty to be with you, but I do not like torture for the sake of torture — remember this."

164

For his eyes, I noticed, were those of a man suffering an acute emotion. I had met his type before: outwardly charming, his characteristics were warping at the promise of blood.

Suddenly Yentin said, "You think I like this?"

"I am beginning to have my suspicions."

"Well, you're wrong. The man's done me no harm." He waved his arms with the mental disarray of one approaching drunken instability, went to the sideboard and filled his glass again, saying, "Damn espionage, damn Hamer and damn that bloody Kwan. Now he is the perfectionist, you realise this? There he sits, Kayling, in the best hotels, giving his orders with a fine dexterity. Gin and vermouth for Kwan To Lin while people like us mop up the blood." He swung to me. "And you're as bad, you realise this? For the kind of information you want I'd have to cut him to pieces."

"That is what he did to Dorothy Ming," I said. "And you are drinking too much."

Into his glass he mumbled, "Dorothy Ming, Jenny Leeshan, Han Moy-tor. . . ."

"You know these names?"

Yentin said, and tears came into his eyes, "I know Hamer."

Going to a drawer in the sideboard he drew out a knife and felt its blade, saying, "But this is no good without the leading questions. Supposing Hamer tells us all this; suppose he gives proof that he has even semi-official support for what he did — if he even did it — would China go to war?"

"I cannot speak for the Central Committee."

"Were the missile launching a complete ship-board accident, for instance, would China retaliate atomically — because of a local accident?"

"I am not her judge. This is politics, not espionage."

"It has a tremendous bearing on the case, you know," he said.

"It has no bearing at all. We are concerned only with getting the truth of how deeply Hamer was politically, if at all, involved."

Yentin was getting drunk, and this was worrying. He was wandering around like a caged tiger now, the knife in his hands, and the sight of it sickened me. True, I had used a knife more than once in my time, but never for torture. In the hands of an expert the knife is the most agonising weapon in espionage. Photographs of Dorothy Ming's body had been circulated freely among First Year students of the School. Hamer, it said, had been with her for sixteen hours, and it was claimed that despite this she had not spoken. But this was not possible. For he had done his work with the skill of a vivisectionist, staunching the flow of her blood with medicaments, the longer to keep her alive. I glanced at Yentin as he approached me. The brightness of his eyes was now quite astonishing, his whole being appearing transfixed with the approaching butchery. He said softly:

"And supposing Hamer talks. Supposing this was a planned attack on Kwangtung, how could China possibly retaliate?"

I emptied my hands at him. "Need we concern ourselves with this?"

"Oh, but it is important, Kayling. We might even be wasting our time on Hamer. China has no rocket method of delivery, not even 'planes capable of a nuclear strike – and that method is as out of date as the war tactics of the Pharaohs."

"She has her methods," I replied.

He crossed the room and drew a port-hole curtain. Over his shoulder, distantly, I saw the red and green mast-head light of Hamer's yacht; more lights blazed from the stern-quarter.

"He is still there," said Yentin. "A woman is due to go aboard at nine. She may be with him when we arrive. You will take care of this woman?"

"Of course."

He said then, "You know of Ku Ata?"

"Who?"

"Ku Ata, the atomic genius and Lum, his assistant."

166

"Who are these people?"

He turned from the port-hole. "You mean to say you have never heard of them? They are Chinese espionage agents; their reputations are international."

I said carelessly, "We, trained in Peking, have no international status, and no knowledge of the stars. Ours is a mundane role, Yentin. Count yourself lucky that you know the people who matter."

"But you surely must have heard of Sea-Entry."

"Of course," I replied.

"And a particular type of Sea-Entry perfected by Ku Ata while he was on the staff of Atomic Research Delivery Methods in Shanghai?"

He took his glass from the sideboard and wandered towards me. I said, "Sea-Entry methods are not unknown, they're practically text-book. In fact, I have often wondered at the astonishing waste of time in perfecting methods of rocket delivery – with all the possibilities of anti-missile interception – when any nation, at any given moment, can explode a device in an enemy country previously brought in by sea."

It was out. It was a speech deliberately long, a fight for time. Yentin was too close to me – barely a foot away. I knew the colour had left my face and I fought the seizing weakness of my knees. Idly I turned, seeking the vital two-pace distance that would give me time to open my handbag, but he was quicker, chopping down with his fist. My handbag fell: stooping, he swiftly snatched it up.

"Scream if you like," he said, "but nobody will hear you."

I stood staring at him. This was not Jan Yentin. *This was Hamer.*

Not with fear, not with horror could I have screamed; only because of the ignomy. I had walked into a web spun by Hamer. Had I planned it, had Kwan himself organised it, it could not have been achieved more thoroughly. Hamer said, draining his glass – and he was now very sober:

"You underrate us. This has always been China's trouble.

The basic fault with Eastern espionage is that it works on an infantile plane. In order to understand the role of the spy one has to be a counter-spy first and understand that role, and China does not."

Names were floating in my mind. Besides Dorothy Ming and Lee-shan and Moy-tor there were three others. One had a name of astonishing beauty, but I remembered only that she was eighteen years old, a terrible age to meet with Hamer. Now he said:

"This kind of thing — it is quite infantile. . . ." Rolling up his cuff he rubbed hard at the tattoo on his left forearm, removing it. "You place too much store on a single, elementary item. . . ."

I said, and do not know why, "Kwan had your photograph, and said it was a photograph of Jan Yentin."

"Kwan was given the wrong photograph — it was one of me. Lin Ho accepted it as readily as you." He looked at his watch. "Poor Pak Lin Ho, we all make mistakes." Taking the gun from my handbag he emptied its shells into his hand, put them into his pocket and said, "But Kwan To Lin lives out his mistakes in the luxury of the Mandarin based on Hong Kong. And the results of his mistakes — the Dorothy Mings, the Jenny Lee-shans and the Mei Kaylings . . . these end up in blood, in hotel rooms or house-boats."

I thought: he will not get a cry from me. If I blunder in the name of China I can at least die decently. The handbag was open on the settee beside him. In the handbag, and he had not yet found it, was the cyanide phial. The sight of it held me with rooted force. As if reading my thoughts he turned the handbag upside down and shook out the phial, putting it into his pocket. Closing my eyes I heard him say:

"We all seek the easy way, Mei Kayling, but there is no easy way for us."

The room tingled with silence. He added:

"Dorothy Ming begged for the cyanide phial, and did not get it. I liked Moy-tor so much better. She was little more than a child, but she begged for nothing."

168

"And Jan Yentin?" I asked.

"There is no earthly reason why I should tell you."

"The sadist usually enjoys his cat and mouse," I said. "You have nothing to lose."

He grunted. "Actually, I didn't handle Yentin, but they tell me he died hard. In the end they got it — the two names — Kayling and Lin Ho. He told us all he knew about you and Lin Ho, but he simply hadn't heard about Lum, Ku Ata — or Sea-Entry."

We stared at each other across the room.

"What are they up to, Kayling — Lum and Ku Ata?"

I sat down against the wall as he rose, the knife in his hand. The onset of torture brings its initial panic before the surge of pain; this, they tell me, is replaced by a creeping coldness, Nature's avenue of escape: ice forms between the brain and the skull. Hamer said, louder, staring down:

"Where are Lum and Ku Ata?"

Sweat was now pouring over my body, my stomach was consumed with sickness.

He was a big man. The weight of the enemy assists the pygmy, in judo. But this would be no street brawl with others intervening. This would be easy for Hamer, with judo, karate, everything in his armament. I smiled up at him.

"Tell me first, did you arrange the bombing of Kwang-tung?"

He sighed. "This is a ludicrous situation."

"Not so ludicrous, Hamer. Surely you owe me the mutual respect of the professional? Satisfy my curiosity and I will talk that much quicker — if I decide to talk at all."

"They all talk," he said.

"We got the negro, you know."

"But not Kurtz."

"We had to leave somebody for your whipping-boy. The negro put us on to you."

"I don't believe it, he didn't guess that much."

"He guessed much more about the House of Representatives."

This stilled him, and was meant to. He said, "Don't tell me I left names lying around.".

"Names that will bring a few down before this business is over."

Hamer licked his lips.

"Take off your dress," he said.

He stood back as I rose from the chair. A nerve, bright blue in his temple, was beating violently, his eyes shining, the pupils dilated into needle points, gleaming black. I said, unbuttoning my dress:

"It was official policy gone wrong, admit it, Hamer."

He was staring at me. His lips moved, making no sound at first, then he said huskily, "Where is Lum, where is Ku Ata?"

"Tell me who you were working for and I will tell you that," I said.

He whispered, "A ship left Osaka on the fourth of May with the man Lum aboard it. She berthed at Shanghai. She sailed from Shanghai on the twenty-fifth after being entered by technicians from Lop Nor, the atomic base in Sinkiang Province. Where is that ship now, where is Lum, where is Ku Ata?"

My dress was in my hands. Reaching out he snatched it from my fingers.

"I will not tell you, Hamer," I said.

For answer he caught my wrist, twisted me across the room, then flung me down on the settee. Still gripping me, he knelt above me, the knife trembling in his hand. "You know of this ship?"

I said, my voice an echo, "I know, but I will not tell you. Do what you did to Dorothy Ming, I will not tell you. But give me the satisfaction of knowing why my province had to die. I lost my people in that explosion. Tell me this, tell me who was behind it, and I will tell you about Lum and Ku Ata — also about the ship."

The grip on my arm went slack. He said huskily, "It's true, then, there is a ship coming on Sea-Entry,"

"It might even be here," I said. "But you don't know where. You don't know what port, what city. Only Lum and Ku Ata and I know that."

He was staring at me, and I shouted into his face:

"You don't know how many ships or how many ports. New Orleans, Texas City, Miami, Philadelphia and New York — and a hundred other places, all sea-board populations, Hamer. All begging for Sea-Entry nuclear attack — the simplest method in the world. And neither you nor Washington know how many ships we have or how many Lums and Ku Atas!"

He stood away from me. His hands were shaking, I noticed. "Your way first, then," he whispered. "And if you talk you'll be the first Chinese agent who has."

I gave a fleeting thought of gratitude to Dorothy Ming, and said:

"Was the attack on Kwangtung deliberate?"

"It was an accident as far as the destroyer was concerned."

"So the drill war-heads and projectors were exchanged for live ones?"

"They were."

"By whom?"

"By me, when I was serving aboard the *Hunter*."

I got up from the settee. "Who was behind you, Hamer?"

He actually smiled. "You could say Big Business."

"Men in the Senate?"

"Not in the Senate."

"But in the House of Representatives?"

"Half Big Business is in the House of Representatives."

"Answer my questions and I'll answer yours, Hamer. How many men?"

"Just one."

"His name?"

"Oh, no, you don't get names."

I shouted, "But why, why? What has China done to him?"

He shouted back, "*Goddam!* What makes you think that everybody loves China?"

"He paid you to do this — although you are an official Government agent, this was work on the side?"

"I was sacked by the C.I.A. — a guy has to live."

"This man you speak of — was he alone in this?"

"He had friends."

"He was acting for Big Business."

"My, you're intelligent."

I said, "Men in the armament trade who are making fortunes out of the Vietnam war and stand to make bigger ones out of an invasion of the Chinese mainland?"

"You're just too intelligent. Now I've got questions. . . ."

I said furiously, "But it was done, first, to provoke China into an attack on Taiwan? The missile could have come from Taiwan, couldn't it? A war between the two Chinas would have rocketed the sales of conventional arms and given America the excuse to invade the China mainland."

"You're answering the questions now, woman, not me."

"But I'm right."

"Sure you're right, but it'll do you no good. Now are you ready for some from me?"

I moved away from Hamer. In the School we are taught to move free of the interrogator if it is possible at the crucial moment. Kwan had said that support would come when I was most desperate; now I was acting according to the rules. I did not know how help would come, in my heart I did not believe help possible. It was only grasping at the straw of Kwan's tremendous ability that made me call, "All right, Kwan, you have heard it all."

I never knew if Ku Ata shot from behind the curtains or if he came into the room, but he made a frightful mess of it, firing, firing before Hamer slowly fell face down. Ku Ata did not speak immediately, but stood astride the dying Hamer and took the silencer off his automatic. Thrusting this into his pocket he pulled out a midget camera.

I began to shake. The appearance of Ku Ata, the

172

intensity of shock and relief made me shake. It began in my legs and flew to my hands, an hysterical, ungovernable shaking.

"Quick," he said, "pull yourself together, woman. Turn him over. I want his face."

Kneeling, I dragged at Hamer. Ku Ata stooped. A little light flashed again and again as the camera clicked, then he said over his shoulder:

"Find the tape-recorder. It's in here somewhere and still running."

I searched the room swiftly and found it, little bigger than a match-box, behind the cocktail cabinet; following its electrical leads I unearthed two tiny microphones, one behind curtains, the other under the settee.

Ku Ata was searching Hamer's pockets for documents. He said, "There must be a switch assembly somewhere – it set the recorder running when you and Hamer came in. Try the door."

At the foot of the door was a minute switch complex, the leads running under the carpet to the cabinet. I pulled it away from the door frame, coiling up its tentacles. Ku Ata, I noticed, had found my automatic and was filling it.

"Is that all?" Gasping, I faced him.

He was stuffing documents into his pockets. "Probably. She gave me a wiring diagram but I think I've lost it – it's not important if we leave anything behind."

"She?"

"Lin Ho. She's the electronic expert, she fixed all this, and also got the master key that let me into here. She made the telephone call from the Roosevelt foyer telling me that you were off to see Hamer. I was in here two minutes before you – she cut it fine."

I stared at him. "Lin Ho?"

He grunted. "She used to be good, but now she's too involved. Children. She makes mistakes, they all make mistakes when they become too involved." He looked at his watch. "By now she'll be on her way to New York. We'd

173

better move. She may not be so good in the hands of the F.B.I. Are you ready?" He pocketed my automatic.

"Of course."

"You're not," he replied, "you haven't got your dress on."

I pulled the dress over my head while his dark eyes moved slowly over me.

"You did well," he said. "I was afraid you'd panic."

"Thank you."

"Kwan set you up as bait, you realise that?"

"I realise that now."

"People like Hamer are paranoiac extroverts. They have to boast to stay alive. Kwan has read his Freud. It was a good team, he and Lin Ho."

"Especially Pak Lin Ho," I said.

Ku Ata opened the door of the boat-house. The masthead lights of Hamer's yacht winked from blackness; rain and cold air struck us in the face.

"What about Hamer's body?" I asked.

"Leave it. No good trying to hide it. People like Hamer live on the lip of life. If he doesn't answer the telephone within fifteen minutes they'll know he's dead."

"And blame Lin Ho."

"That's what she's there for," Ku Ata said.

CHAPTER EIGHTEEN

Ku Ata had a car parked on South Side. Within half-an-hour of leaving Hamer's house-boat on the Monongahela we were averaging a steady sixty miles an hour on the road to Cleveland. Sitting beside Ku Ata I examined him in the faint green light of the dashboard: it was difficult to believe that behind his flat profile existed the brain of one of the best espionage men in the world, a brain that also embraced within its fantastic scope the genius of the top scientist. He was a small man, a few inches over five feet tall, his conversation sparse and monosyllabic, rather as if it were being executed by a minute portion of a brain, leaving the larger, more important section for problems of greater interest than Mei Kayling, minor agent. The deserted road swept lazily upon us in a white blaze of light, the black tree-fringe above us raced over an avenue of stars.

"You have the camera?" he asked.

"Yes."

"Take out the film roll most carefully and put it in your handbag." He switched off the dashboard light, slowed his speed and turned the lights to parking.

I did this, fingers fumbling in my lap.

The headlights blazed, the night made shape again. Ku Ata said, "Take the tape out of the recorder and wrap it against damage; put this in your handbag also."

It began to rain in sudden wind-shriek, sweeping in diadems of water across the black, forbidding country. Beaver Falls flashed by in glistening mist, drenched roofs winking dismally at a storm-tossed moon.

"You are awake, Mei Kayling?" Ku Ata said later.

"I am awake."

"Excellent. It is necessary, according to the brief, that you should dye your hair."

"Kwan To Lin did not mention this possibility," I said.

"Kwan To Lin may not have considered the possibility of Lin Ho breaking down. Hair the colour of yours, bright golden, could be a personal ticket to the F.B.I."

"You have the dye?"

He handed me a little phial. "The dye powder is here, the last service of Lin Ho. Water you have in plenty. I will stop at the next convenient place. With the heater full on, your hair should be dry before we reach Cleveland."

"And at Cleveland?" I asked.

"You will catch the 11-40 p.m. plane to San Francisco, via Kansas City."

"And you, Ku Ata?"

He slowed the car, turning it expertly into a lay-by. "Here is a convenient place to dye your hair, Mei Kayling."

175

From the boot of the car he gave me a bowl. Kneeling above this bowl with my fine bright hair dangling before me, lashed by rain and wind, I dyed my hair black while Ku Ata, in the shelter of the car, smoked with the nonchalance of a Peking merchant. I was beginning to dislike him.

"And at San Francisco?" I asked, now seated beside him, wrapping my hair in a towel. "What happens there?"

He changed gear in a sudden gush of water from the flooded highway; light sprayed, rain pelted the windscreen. He replied, "At San Francisco you fly to Tokyo — you are a fashion house representative returning from a business trip. You have your passport handy?"

"Here." I held it up and he took it, slipping it into his pocket.

"In exchange, one from Old Man." He gave me another passport. "The hair changes colour, the passports alter. Flight tickets you will find inside. Nothing is forgotten."

"And you?" I asked again.

He took a deep breath. "There is, in San Francisco harbour, a town called San José. Its population, they tell me, is roughly equivalent to that of Hoon, north-east of Canton in Kwangtung Province. Both towns, as you know, are close to a sea-board."

"There you have a rendezvous with Lum?"

He nodded. "Who is on the ship that sailed from Osaka."

I said, faintly, "This is Sea-Entry."

"Did the Americans consider this when they rocketed the village of Hoon?"

I said quickly, "But Sea-Entry was never perfected . . ."

"It has been now. Yesterday Lum's ship anchored off San Francisco harbour, near San José."

"Waiting to be detonated?" I stared at him in the faint light. "On whose authority?"

"We await that authority."

I said hotly, "But you will never get it. If that authority is dependent upon my report it will never come. My report, based on the photograph and the Hamer recording, will make it perfectly clear. The Kwangtung disaster was never backed by the American Government, it was backed and organised by the very opposite – the enemies of America."

"But Americans nevertheless," said Ku Ata.

I answered, "If you are going to sit in San Francisco harbour and wait for a Chinese decision to atom-bomb this sea-board, you will wait for a very long time."

"We may be hotheads, Lum and I, but we are patriots, Mei Kayling. The decision belongs to the Central Committee. We will not anticipate it. If the decision, based upon your report, is a negative one, we will bring Sea-Entry back to Osaka in the normal manner."

I stared through the windscreen.

Ku Ata spoke again, saying, "Sea-Entry makes nonsense of this anti-missile rubbish. While their armament kings are making millions out of fantastic schemes for home protection, the American people are being hoodwinked. One does not need rockets to atom-bomb her ports, and this America will learn."

I asked, "So Sea-Entry is not confined to San Francisco?"

"Of course not. Bombs have been planted in various American ports over the last two years. Once you get them in by Sea-Entry there's a score of ways of planting them – over the ship's side and into the mud, lowered into submerged wrecks, chained by anchor off the harbours, down coastal mineshafts. Detonation can be effected electronically, by radio signal, or by a timed device with manual actuation. Have you heard of Thermo-Port-Reaction?"

I said I had not.

Ku Ata continued, "This is total retaliation – a chain-reaction based on home news reports. As news of one disaster comes in another bomb is detonated by an agent elsewhere. Simplicity is the key: the attacked country subscribes to her own destruction, as it were. Once chain-detonation has begun, it cannot be stopped, of course."

"It sounds ingenious," I said softly. "You had a hand in this?"

177

He smiled. "I conceived it, I designed it."

"But you would not detonate without written instructions?"

He replied, "I am a scientist, Kayling. The fact that I am of Japanese blood, that my country was devastated by the American atom bombs, that my parents died in Hiroshima, has no bearing on my actions. The act of detonating the San Francisco Sea Entry will be my responsibility, but I will not authorise it without written instructions."

It was sheer ego, of course. China would never vest in one man such terrifying authority.

Ku Ata said, for no apparent reason:

"If Sea-Entry is detonated the Americans will have no cause for complaint."

I glanced at him, and he continued, "This accidental rocketing of Kwangtung Province is the logical outcome of their military aggressions — with a nation as trigger-happy as this one a mistake had to come eventually — but there is much more to it than this. American containment of Communism runs from north to south of China's coast; arrows from the atomic Polaris aim at our heart; Chiang Kai-shek, supported by Washington, bristles over Quemoy; from the islands of Japan south to Hong Kong we are threatened by the American Seventh Fleet; in Vietnam they play with fire."

I answered, "This is politics, Ku Ata: we are concerned with espionage."

Ignoring this, he said, "Now consider what America would do were the situation reversed — just consider it! Supposing a Chinese fleet, based, say, on the Bahamas, was supporting an army of rebel Americans led by a defecting ex-President who planned to invade the American mainland ... Are you listening?"

"Certainly."

"And supposing this same Chinese fleet sailed year after year off the American sea-board from Miami to New

York, with rockets aimed at her great cities — then you would have an exact parallel to the Taiwan situation, you agree?"

"Entirely," I replied.

Ku Ata took a deep breath. "In such a situation of confrontation, what would America do?"

"Go to war." I added, "But why are you asking me this?"

He shrugged. "It is interesting to get a second opinion. Go to war — that is exactly what China is about to do."

"I doubt it," I said.

"Do not be too sure, Mei Kayling, do not be too sure."

He stared through the streaming glass at the yellow road.

I said, later, "The Americans have cleared the Osaka ship in San Francisco?"

"Have they an option? Their import trade would cease overnight if they were to examine every ship for a possible atomic device. The difficulty, from our point of view, has always been the method of detonation."

"This must be done from the land?"

Ku Ata said, "Until recently this was the requirement, and it was not only cumbersome but liable to detection. Radio actuation comes direct from Peking, based on a code; this code energises the servo-manual device necessary for remote detonation. Lum merely receives the radio code and feeds it into a computer."

It was inhuman and sad: these faceless pawns in the game of war.

"A sort of transistorised puppet?"

"Lum is incredible."

"Lum is a fanatic," I said.

Ku Ata sighed. "In the Japanese war against American aggression our peasant soldiers used to sit in slit trenches with a land mine between their knees and a stone poised, waiting for the American tanks. Lum is a good scientist, but he is the first one we have trained who is prepared to do the same."

179

"Where is the device?"

Ku Ata peered through the streaming window at advancing cross-roads and swung the wheel. I saw a phantom sign-post and a frantic waving of wayside trees.

"Should you know this?" he asked.

"Sea-Entry methods are normal teaching — even the Americans realise the hazards. The subject is intensely interesting."

He said, "In this case a simple steel blister is built externally on the hull of the ship below the water-line, and the device is housed in there. To offset drag on the hull, which would necessitate constant rudder correction, a similar blister is attached on the starboard side. In this one the operator lives."

"In this case, Lum."

He nodded. "Simple electronic connections between operator and device are built in, the ship itself being used for the positive side of these connections. With sea-drag counteracted even the helmsman is not aware that the blisters are fitted."

"An escape route for the operator?"

"There is no escape route for the operator. The present design is based on a detonation drill that is purely suicidal, though there is an egress hatch on the hull side which allows the operator entry into the cargo hull."

"To avoid claustrophobia?"

"Exactly. Even for a man as dedicated as Lum this was an insurmountable problem. Hysteria pestered him after two weeks of total isolation. Hope is a necessary ingredient for combating claustrophobia, and in this case there is no hope. Much as I contested it, the wander-hatch was incorporated. I contested this initially on the basis that a twenty-four-hour radio watch was inevitable to the success of the operation. All calls received by the ship must be monitored by the blister operator. Absence from the blister for even a moment might mean loss of the one call that is operational."

"It sounds efficient."

"Under conditions of trial we found it efficient providing the operator was not contained for longer than eighteen days. When all you can offer a man at the end of eighteen days' solitary confinement is instant vapourising, it becomes a test of the man, to say the least."

My hair was dry. With the aid of the sun-mirror I combed it into long, black waves, and unaccountably began to wonder if the negro would like it the colour of jet. I remembered how he used to love my hair, running his thick fingers through its gold. I remembered, also, the bright sands of Coloane, the stuttering panic of the sea-birds, the crash of the breakers and the translucent, warping body of Joe the Cormorant as he raced over oceans of sea-flora and bright pink shells, the treasure of the islands. And I recalled, with growing coldness, that the negro's family lived in San Francisco; that the three-second detonating wave of ten billion candle-power would blaze about their tenement slum, enter the kitchen where they ate, the hall where his mother had borne her children. Revulsion beset me with increasing intensity, and I stared at Ku Ata in the faint green light of the dashboard: I did not trust Ku Ata.

His face, the complete Oriental: the face of the rapists of Hong Kong, of the fanatical 'banzai!', was inscrutable. I saw in this face the prostitution of Shanghai and the flames of Nanking; I saw the cinder-pit of a town once called San José. Suddenly Ku Ata said:

"We have worked together, Mei Kayling. It would be less than loyal if I did not tell you that you stand in some disgrace."

"I do not know what you mean," I said softly.

"There will be no adulation when you return to Peking."

My heart began to hit against my body. Sweat, my old enemy, beaded my forehead. With a light gesture I smoothed it into my hair. Ku Ata said:

"Life is basically unfair. It is the safe ones sitting at home who get the approbation. In this profession, if we are successful, they make a minor gesture of approval; if we fail publicly, death can be preferable."

"What are you trying to say?"

"That Kwan has been recalled to Peking."

I sat up in the seat. "I do not believe it!"

"There is more than a hint, apparently, of a moral transgression. . . ."

"This is known of Kwan. This is not news."

He moved impatiently. "It is not news all the time the Party winks at it. Is it not part of the ethics of our Cultural Revolution that people should improve their state, physically, morally, socially? Kwan has not improved. He is characteristically immoral. Investigation naturally follows, and Kwan's amours do not stand investigation."

I closed my eyes. "I understand."

"You might do, but do you see the repercussions?"

"I am beginning to."

"This is the fault of brilliance, Kayling. It sheds a warm glow, it enmeshes, ensnares and finally traduces. There are women involved, apparently."

"And I am one?"

Ku Ata said, "It is hardly sufficient to claim you loved him, though officialdom can be human also, give it credit. But on the eve of an operation of this importance, Kayling, it was scarcely diplomatic, to say the least."

"The keeper of the lodging-house, in Peking?"

He nodded. "You talked to her of Su Shiun?"

I replied hotly. "I talked to her of Communism. If my memory serves me correctly, she was a particularly bad Communist."

"She had a particularly good memory, she has reported you." He sighed. "This, as you know, is revisionism."

"It is inhumanity," I said.

"That will be for the Ministry of Social Security to judge."

I sat in silence, screwing my hands in my lap. It was the appalling disgrace that tortured me. China would indict me as undesirable. Now, in retrospect, I knew it was a terrible insult to China's virtue. I bowed my head. Ku Ata continued:

"Other views may prevail, of course. In the performance of one's duty an act of blatant immorality can be deemed sacrifice. Yours is the guilt because yours is the strength. Men are weak. You are a lovely woman. Because I am a man, I am much in sympathy with Kwan. For you I hold only a deep disdain."

This would not mean death of the body, only death of the spirit. When I returned they would send me to a school for thought-correction. The mind rehabilitated was often the best, the purest. Ku Ata was speaking, but I did not hear him. I was remembering the agony of the giant from Huhehot and the animal gasps of Yuen Sun Johnny. I remembered, too, the man of Coloane. Some things they could take from me, but never this. Yet I deserved such punishment. My behaviour with Kwan in the glow of my country's confidence was unforgivable.

Ku Ata said suddenly, "I have broken the code, Mei Kayling."

"I do not understand."

He said, "The Peking detonation code. I have broken it."

I closed my eyes, thankful for the darkness. "Since ... since you now know the code you can feed the information into Lum's computer?"

"Exactly."

"Then you can detonate Sea-Entry in San Francisco?"

I knew he was testing me. Sweat was upon his face. Obviously he was suffering a tremendous emotion, a man being crucified by his own obliterating sense of power. Taking a deep breath, "Of course," he replied.

"And do you intend to do so without official permission?"

"Possibly."

"That is no answer. Do you intend to detonate or not?"

This I said, hearing my voice as an echo. Ice was in my throat; my hands began to tremble and I gripped them in my lap. Ku Ata said:

183

"You are not appalled?"

"Why should I be? It is an open and shut case of American aggression. We have the evidence."

"What do you mean by that?"

He stared at me. If it had been his intention to humiliate and cow me he had not been successful. I said, "I mean that you will undoubtedly get instructions to detonate on the evidence we hold. It is inevitable. Unless China makes a positive act of retaliation some other bright faction on the edge of the White House lawn will take the opportunity to rocket us again despite official American fury."

He stared again, as if in disbelief. "You really believe this?"

"Of course."

"But that is a complete reversal of the attitude you took half-an-hour ago."

"My future has also suffered a complete reversal," I replied. "Besides, if Lin Ho breaks down they will unearth Lum and disarm the Osaka ship. Sea-Entry would be condemned for the next generation, and it is the only bargaining power China has got."

He said eagerly, and I knew I had got him, "Then you agree to anticipate the Peking decision?"

"This is a local problem, Ku Ata. On reflection there is simply not time to refer it back. The men on the ground are the men in power. Put this in the hands of the home-based politicians and they'll waste a fortnight confirming a formal issue. Will Lin Ho last that long?"

"They wasted less time on Nagasaki," he said softly.

His eyes, I noticed, were mere shadows in his face.

"They wasted even less on Hiroshima," I said, watching him.

The night flew on in blustering wind; the needle of the speedometer wavered around ninety miles an hour. I lay back in my seat, pretending to sleep, my brain tuned to every movement about me. Youngstown splashed past in a rising flood of rain, her sodden highways glimmering under a misted moon. Calculating that Cleveland airport was about half-an-hour ahead I said, with feigned tiredness:

"Where are we?"

"Just north of Warren. At this rate you should catch the 'plane with about ten minutes to spare."

"And you, Ku Ata?"

"I will give you time to get out of America, then contact Lum. The explosion is a direct reprisal — two megatons — no more, no less than the explosion in Kwangtung."

"They have no cause for complaint," I said.

"Not least do I appreciate your co-operation in this, Kayling. When one is determined on a path of action there is little need for moral support, yet it is good to know that you agree with me."

"It is a very human reaction."

"Needless to say, you will be repaid. I will speak for you when I reach Peking. Your behaviour while with me has been exemplary."

It was astonishing naïveté. "Thank you," I said, and glanced at my watch. "We must be near. I will get my suitcase out of the back", and knelt, reaching over into the back seat with my right hand. As I did this I retrieved my automatic from his coat pocket with my fine left hand, levelled it, and said:

"Pull off the road, Ku Ata."

I think he knew, without a glance at me, exactly what had happened, yet only his hands betrayed him, the knuckles cutting white on the steering-wheel: this was all a part of the game. Friends became enemies on a chance remark, counter-action following with heartless rapidity.

"Kayling. . . ."

"Pull off the road," I said. I levelled the automatic at his head.

I knew exactly what he would do. He would attack the moment he had the car under easier control, so I shot as he slowed it towards the kerbside. As he fell I pushed him

185

against the door, switched off the ignition and reached over for the hand-brake, steering the car to a halt. Wind and rain lashed the windows. Leaping out, I stared up and down the deserted highway. Distantly, a headlight beamed from the direction of Warren. Ku Ata slid easily into my arms as I opened the driver's door. For a moment I held him; there was on his face a strange, unearthly peace.

"Oh no, Ku Ata," I said, "you must wait for China."

He was unexpectedly light, even for a small man. Dragging him round the car I laid his body in the roadside ditch, first taking from his pockets all identifying papers: storm water flooded over his face, I remember, as I covered him with thick bracken.

Leaping back into the car, I accelerated along the road towards Cleveland.

CHAPTER NINETEEN

It was three minutes past midday. The white buildings of San Francisco airport blazed in the noonday sun. The big Pan-American jet accelerated along the tarmac in clubbing blasts of air. Around me sat the passengers, in that tightened couldn't-care-less that always pervades a take-off, the brandy revellers in the front seats hunched in a gloom of alcoholic inevitability, secretly contemplating the horror of death by fire. And below us, slanting skywards, San Francisco crashed and fumed in its unknown last minute reprieve from blindness. Ghosts sat about me. Lum I saw first, sitting in his blister in the hull of Sea-Entry, awaiting the shift of his finger on the button, eyes wide in expectation of the searing light, a split second agony of fire before his brain was decimated by skull splinters, and vapourised. Lum was brave, I reflected. It took more than mere fanaticism to count the fortnight in seconds before such a horrifying death. Pak Lin Ho came to me next, her hair awry, face blood-stained, staring into the arcing lamp which men call Truth, playing her role of The

Bright Cantonese. If the timing was right Lin Ho had already been several hours in the hands of the F.B.I. Vaguely, I wondered if she would last until I left Hong Kong. And Kwan. How clearly I saw Kwan at his indolent, arrogant worst, parading his bourgeois immorality, face lifted in defiance before the elders of the Presidium who had forgotten their youth too soon. Soon I should join him in this parade. A six months' course at the School of Correction was degradation enough for me, but for Kwan this would mean moral death, for he priced dignity high. I pitied him. Then came the faces of Yentin and Hamer, the killed and the killer, side by side, these two, in the eye of my mind; friends, indeed, each sanctified by love of country, a thought or frown on the face of his nation. Old Man came next, his old face collapsing into a thousand wrinkles, sipping his Caselhino wine beneath the bahuina trees of the *Praia Grande*. And in his shadow stood the dying Ku Ata.

An instant, flying thought for Ku Ata, for remembering Old Man brought me memories of the negro. I sat up in my seat, eyes closed.

Let this be known, though it is never believed: my country does not kill for the sake of killing, so this negro would not die, whatever Old Man's threats and Lin Ho's suggestions. If he was in China, then I would go instantly to China. But if he was still on Coloane then I would beg of Old Man the grace of two hours of freedom and take the white ferry to the fish-gamble. If my gods served me, then Richard might be waiting.

The thought of him brought me to a pitch of tremendous joy.

Twisting my hands in my lap, I remembered Coloane; clenching my eyes to the glare of the sun I knew again the stupefying heat of the fish-gamble, the shattering brightness of the beach where the mare's skull grinned on the totem-pole; smelled again the sea-salt, seaweed, rotting smell of dismembered crab and clawed lobster; felt the arms of Richard about me, his body enmeshed in mine.

"I love you," I said, but none heard this.

The 'plane droned on. The sea thirty thousand feet below was cobalt blue and glorious, running for the eternity of waste, flanked with great wash-day cumulus clouds boiling in crescendo billowings against a sky of incinerating glare; and I suddenly hated Ku Ata and was glad that he had died. For if this beauty was to be sullied by a mushroom cloud, if this glorious sea-board was to be stunned and blinded, it would happen by China's will, after discussion, after consideration by the greatest brains in China, not by the whim of a single individual, Japanese blood-tie at that. Who was Ku Ata to judge the time and manner of retaliation? Or was his a retaliation for Nagasaki and Hiroshima? Let my country plan her destiny, and be my judge. Let her punish me for immorality, but not for the murder of one like Ku Ata.

Then my thoughts became happier, for I again remembered the negro.

If I am rejected by China, I thought, I will go to Macau and there live with him, for assuredly he would be rejected by America. There in the fish-gamble we would live, Richard and I, and in years to come the tourists visiting Coloane would say, "See those strange children! Look – do you see those children playing in the surf? They are not Chinese because the Chinese skin is golden. They are neither Ports nor Macanese because of the colour of their eyes. Mozambiques, you say? How can they be Mozambiques in such numbers? Are the pataca girls down the *Beca da Roza* so careless in their loving? One or two have a strange pigment of the skin, you notice. Hoklo? Not the ferocious Hoklo or charming Tan-gar because these are a little tribe, their limbs tiny. No, these are children of the sun. Rather as if they sprang from the loins of a blonde English girl and an American negro. Children of bright hair and black bodies, the glorious Afro-Nordic Eurasians!"

I thought, smiling, only the most searching enquiries would get at the truth: that once, long ago, there lived

188

together in a fish-gamble on Coloane beach a giant American negro and a Red Guard Second Class Chinese albino.

Soon I would land in Kai Tak, Hong Kong. I knew what would happen there, for I had seen it happen before. There would be a bowed greeting, smiles that hid the official stares of disapproval. There would be a waiting car, probably black, three black-suited Chinese business men, and a driver. One man would sit in the front of the car, two would sit at the back with me in the middle: scrupulously polite, most kind to me, even on the road that led to Canton. I should not be tortured for confession, as the rest of the world would have us believe; I should suffer no unkindness. I should merely stand in the hall of the Presidium, and a man would call:

"Red Guard Second Class, the woman Mei Kayling."

I thought then:

You may indict me for my immorality with Kwan To Lin, you may call me a paramour. But you will never know the torture of the giant man of Huhehot, the dreadful indignity of Yuen Sun Johnny.

Nor will you, my beloved China, ever learn of the love I bear for my negro on Coloane. In the School of Correction this comes under no rule of confession, no curriculum.

We had been flying for only about ten minutes when I opened my eyes to reality. Two hostesses were serving morning coffee, I think, for there was much chattering and laughter among the passengers, and a rattle of crockery.

And then it happened.

One of the hostesses was standing by my aisle seat. I saw her face, it was a most beautiful face, crowned with dark hair. She was laughing, her head back, and the laughter of her eyes changed slowly into perplexity.

She was looking towards the tail of the 'plane.

A strange light began to glow about her, brighter, brighter. People rose in their seats, I remember, their faces horrified.

And the light beamed into an arc-light intensity, so that I involuntarily covered my eyes.

Somewhere in the 'plane a woman began to scream in rhythmic shrieks, higher, higher, in shrill notes, like a child being mutilated. And still the light burned on, then slowly died. Turning in my seat I stared towards San Francisco.

A mushroom cloud was forming over the city.

Later, reading through Ku Ata's papers, I saw his coded message to Peking. It was brief: "Attack on Kwangtung deliberate U.S. policy. Recorded proof coming via 1869681. Further U.S. nuclear attacks on China sea-board imminent. Imperative to make Chinese reprisal by Sea-Entry on San José: advised time 1210 hrs. July 13th. *Ack.*"

This message had been radioed an hour before I met Hamer. Ku Ata, they discovered too late, was born in Hiroshima: it was a mistake from which the Ministry of Social Security (Personnel Branch) might never recover, situated as it was in the middle of Peking.

The 'plane bucked to the arrival of the explosion blast, dived, and bucked again. People were screaming. To keep my composure I took out my compact and powdered my nose. The captain was vainly trying to tell us that he was flying on to Tokyo, and that by the look of it something dreadful was happening to San Francisco.

He was understating the case.

Now it was twelve minutes since Sea-Entry had exploded, and it was up to Lin Ho. Strange, I reflected, that my fate should depend so utterly on Pak Lin Ho. They would get the truth out of her eventually, of course: they always got the truth eventually: in this particular art we are all as bad as one another.

Vaguely, I wondered if it was worth going on to Peking.

Later still I learned that China did not confine herself to San Francisco. In expectation of further American attacks, Peking's Thermo-Port-Reaction time-table was as follows:

'San Francisco 2 megatons, 1211 hrs. New Orleans 8 megatons, 1243 hrs. Los Angeles 6 megatons, 1250 hrs. Miami 18 megatons, 1305 hrs. Philadelphia 20 megatons, 1318 hrs. Boston 9 megatons, 1321 hrs. New York and Washington 28 megatons (simultaneously), 1338 hrs.'

There were many others, of course, forming a belt around the United States: I do not remember how many others there were, but I know it worked out to thirty-eight million American dead.

It was now a push-button world, I thought, sitting there among the shrieking passengers, but Macau would probably be a long way from the hypocentres, and, after all, I was practically a free agent.

With luck my Richard might still be on Coloane.

EPIC FICTION FROM CORONET

ALEXANDER CORDELL

	15476 4	The Sinews of Love	80p
	17403 X	The Fire People	£1.00
	20515 6	Rape of the Fair Country	85p
	20509 1	Hosts of Rebecca	85p
	20516 4	Song of the Earth	85p

EILIS DILLON

| | 18802 2 | Across the Bitter Sea | £1.25 |

JOHN CREASEY

| | 20801 5 | The Masters of Bow Street | £1.25 |

MALCOLM MACDONALD

| | 20010 3 | World from Rough Stones | £1.00 |

All these books are available at your local bookshop or newsagent, or can be ordered direct from the publisher. Just tick the titles you want and fill in the form below.

Prices and availability subject to change without notice.

– – – – – – – – – – – – – – – – – – – –

CORONET BOOKS, P.O. Box 11, Falmouth, Cornwall.

Please send cheque or postal order, and allow the following for postage and packing:

U.K. – One book 18p plus 8p per copy for each additional book ordered, up to a maximum of 66p.

B.F.P.O. and EIRE – 18p for the first book plus 8p per copy for the next 6 books, thereafter 3p per book.

OTHER OVERSEAS CUSTOMERS – 20p for the first book and 10p per copy for each additional book.

Name ....

Address ....

....

....